Praise for Laurie Paige:

"Laurie Paige doesn't miss…"
—*New York Times* bestselling author
Catherine Coulter

"Fan-favorite Laurie Paige has created her
strongest and most engaging work to date."
—*Affaire de Coeur* on *Father Found*

"It is always a joy to savor the consistent
excellence of this outstanding author."
—*Romantic Times*

"A dazzling display of creativity. The variation
on a standard plot is extremely fresh, with superb
characterization to carry it off. Readers will hang
on the edge wondering how the situation can be
resolved, but Ms. Paige comes up trumps with
a thoroughly satisfying resolution."
—*Romantic Times* on *Nothing Lost*

"Laurie Paige weaves engaging characters and tender
emotions into interesting situations and comes up
with a good, solid love story every time.
Enjoy the magic of Laurie Paige!"
—Kathleen Eagle, Romance Writers of America
RITA® Award Winner

THE FORTUNES OF TEXAS: Reunion

LAURIE PAIGE
Lone Star Rancher

Silhouette Books

Published by Silhouette Books
America's Publisher of Contemporary Romance

Special thanks and acknowledgment are given
to Laurie Paige for her contribution
to THE FORTUNES OF TEXAS: REUNION series.

 SILHOUETTE BOOKS

LONE STAR RANCHER

Copyright © 2005 by Harlequin Books S.A.

ISBN 0-373-38929-9

Visit Silhouette Books at www.eHarlequin.com

Printed in U.S.A.

Dear Reader,

Part of the fun of making up stories is imagining
yourself in the environment. Having lived in Austin,
it was easy to imagine the ranching country and
sweeping vistas of Texas for the Flying Aces ranch.
When Jessica hiked along the creek, I walked with
her. When she checked the eggs for twin yolks, I
remembered being six again and visiting my uncle's
egg barn. I also recall quite clearly being pecked by
an irritated hen when I ruffled her feathers.

Writing Jessica and Clyde's story took me back to
Ryan Fortune and his family. I was delighted to find
that his twin daughter, Vanessa, was happy in her
marriage, and that all had worked out well with the
missing baby. (Did I mention that I get really involved
in my characters' lives?) Sometimes readers ask what
happened to so-and-so in one of our fictional families.
I enjoy exploring the possibilities with them. Life is
full of twists and turns, and that's the joy of writing:
one gets a chance to explore the "road less traveled."

Laurie Paige

For Grandpa, Ryan and Kevin—
It was fun camping with you guys!

One

Jessica Miller sighed in relief as she entered the dim cool-ness of the restaurant. Outside the temperature was in the nineties, not unusual for early August in New York City.

She was aware of the glances and outright stares when she followed the restaurant hostess to the table where her best friend waited for her. At five-ten and wearing sandals with two-inch heels, Jessica was tall enough to be a high-fashion model and, in fact, that was how she made her living.

With wide, bright blue eyes and light brown hair that needed little enhancement to make her look like a summer blonde, she had a face well known to the public.

"Jessica, I'm so glad you're here," her friend Violet For-tune said. "I was afraid the photo shoot wouldn't be finished."

"I told the director it had to be because I was leaving at noon." She wrinkled her nose, then smiled at her old chum from long-ago summer vacations and college days.

Violet and her family were from New York but they had

visited their Fortune cousins in Texas each summer at the Double Crown Ranch outside Red Rock, which was near San Antonio. Jessica's father had managed the local hardware store in Red Rock, and Jessica had been born and raised in the small town. The girls had met as youngsters and formed a solid friendship.

They'd shared a room at college the first year, then Jessica had been discovered by the owner of a top New York modeling agency. The woman had attended a college function with her niece, spotted Jessica and demanded to represent her in a modeling career. Since the hardware store was going out of business and Jessica knew her parents and younger sister would need income, she'd taken the offer, given up her scholarship and moved to the city.

But only after the agency owner had promised Jessica's father she would guard his daughter from the predatory worms in the Big Apple who would devour fresh-faced country girls for a snack.

For the first two years of her new life in the city Jessica had actually lived in Sondra's home—with Sondra's son, five-year-old Bertram, whose father was a diplomat stationed in France; Mutley, the dog who'd followed Bertie home from the park; and four assorted cats.

At twenty-one, she'd decided she was old enough to be on her own and had bought her first New York apartment, which was where she'd lived for the past twelve years.

The other condos she owned were rented, as were the parking spaces she'd bought on the second floor of the parking garage next to her place. All in all, the country gal had done well. She was one of the three top-paid models in the world, according to *Forbes* magazine.

"What are you snickering about?" Violet demanded as Jessica took a seat opposite her friend.

"Life," Jessica said.

Violet gave an exaggerated shrug. "Oh, that."

The two friends laughed merrily. However, there were undertones of sadness in Violet's eyes.

Jessica refrained from questioning her friend, but she knew the sadness had to do with work. After Violet had finished medical school and residency requirements, she'd taken advanced training in neurology and settled in the city, too. She'd stayed with Jessica for a few months before finding her own place. Brilliant at diagnosing brain disorders, she was well known for her pioneering studies.

Recently Violet had been the chief physician or consulting expert on several very difficult cases. While Jessica hadn't understood the intricacy of the diseases when they had discussed the problems, she'd recognized her friend's sense of failure whenever a patient didn't make it.

Jessica thought this was taking a serious toll on the skillful, sensitive doctor, but it did no good to tell Violet the tragedies weren't her fault. She knew that, and that she had to find her own emotional balance—

"Uh, excuse me, Ms. Miller, but, uh, could I have your autograph?" a young, feminine voice interrupted.

Jessica held her smile in place. Although she wished people would leave her in peace when she was about her private business, her career precluded that possibility.

Sondra had explained all that before letting her sign a contract with the agency. Her agent was a stickler for being polite to the public, who, after all, contributed to the success of her career.

"Of course," Jessica said. "What's your name? Are you visiting the city or do you live here?"

The teenager was obviously delighted that the famous

model was talking to her. Jessica wrote the girl's name and a brief message and signed the spiral-bound notebook. Ten other people lined up at once.

The restaurant owner was adept at handling this sort of thing. He stopped others from joining the line and, after Jessica had autographed various pieces of paper, shooed the guests to their seats and reminded them that Ms. Miller also had to eat.

"Now I recall why I was reluctant to have my picture in the medical journal with that article on long-term diseases of the brain," Violet said with a wry grimace when they were alone.

"Yes." Jessica sighed as she looked over the menu.

After they'd ordered, Violet narrowed her eyes and studied her friend. "So," she said, leaning in to the table, "are you going to tell me what's happening?"

Jessica grimaced. "I have a slight problem." She hesitated to mention it in view of the life-and-death struggles her friend dealt with every day.

"Yes?" Violet drew the word out.

"There's a local politician, a semi-biggie, who's, uh, sort of stalking me. I think."

Violet's manner became dead serious. "Who is it? Do you know? What's he doing?"

"Roy Balter. I met him at a weekend party. I couldn't take a step without falling over him. He asked for a date. I declined by saying my time was already spoken for. That usually discourages unwanted attention. But not with him. He repeatedly asked to see me."

"What happened next?"

"When I returned to the city, it started out with flowers. Tons of them every day. After the first few, I refused to accept any others. Now it's phone calls."

"Demanding to see you?"

"No. Heavy breathing. When he first started calling my private line and wanting to meet for dinner or the theater, I changed the number. He got the new one, but now he doesn't say anything when he calls."

"Oh." Her friend thought it over. "How do you know it's him?"

"Feminine intuition and the fact that the telephone number is blocked from identification."

Violet looked somewhat dubious. "I see."

"I talked to the district judge, but without solid evidence, he can't issue a restraining order. The police have informed me that without one they can't do a thing, even if the man is in my building. He has to be *in* my condo."

Jessica shuddered at the thought of him invading her private space. For the first time she admitted to herself that she was a tiny bit frightened by his persistence. It seemed obsessive…vindictive, even.

"You're sure it's him?"

"Positive. Sometimes he gives this little laugh just before he hangs up. I recognized it from the three days at the house party. It became quite annoying."

"When he stayed glued to your side," Violet concluded.

"Right."

"Stalkers are dangerous. We need to do something."

The nice thing about having a best friend like Violet was her willingness to take on another's problems and plant herself in the middle of them. It had been Violet who had helped her fill out scholarship forms for college and prodded her when she'd felt discouraged.

"You're too smart to settle down to a mediocre marriage and life in a small town. It'll stifle you," her mentor had told her with the confidence of being eighteen and an honor graduate of a prestigious prep school.

Jessica had held the second-highest grade point average

in her graduating class, but that had been in Red Rock, and hadn't counted for much, or so she had thought. Violet had disagreed and persuaded her to go for the gold, which in her case was a scholarship to study economics.

She really would have preferred classical guitar, but she didn't think many people made a living at that. Her duty had been to her family.

However, because of the money she made from modeling, she had become interested in the investment world and had taken classes to qualify as a financial advisor for the day when her modeling career would be over. At thirty-three, she was lucky to still be on top.

Violet snapped her fingers, startling Jessica out of her introspection. "I know," she said.

"Know what?"

"What you should do."

"Oh, yeah?" Jessica asked. "Is this anything like your brainstorm when we were sixteen that we should go down to Galveston, collect sand fleas and sell them to fishermen in order to make a fortune, only we ended up with a bucket of rotten little critters that no one wanted?"

Violet gave her a mock stern frown. "Of course not. This is serious." Her tone was light, but her eyes looked worried, making Jessica sorry she'd mentioned the problem. "I think you should go to Texas—"

"No way. That might put my parents in danger. And my sister and her family."

"Let me finish. You should go to Texas and stay with my brothers at their ranch. No one will find you there. When your stalker realizes you're gone, he'll give up."

Jessica wanted to believe that. "Why would he?"

"He gets his satisfaction from taunting you. If that stops, he'll move on."

"Right, to some other unlucky woman."

Her friend nodded, her manner sympathetic. "That's the way the world works, unfortunately."

Their food came. Jessica murmured her thanks to the waitress, then gazed at Violet. "I can't leave the city now. I have a full schedule until the end of the month. I had planned to take September and October off, though, before heading to Italy for a special swimsuit layout."

"It'll be cold in November," Violet reminded her.

"Tell me about it. We'll be filming in the Alps, if you can believe that." She started on her chicken salad. "So how's it going on the medical front? Any miracle cures I should know about?"

"I wish. I'm thinking of taking a cruise in the South Seas or something equally wild and extravagant."

"Ha," Jessica said, knowing her friend rarely took a day off, much less a whole week or more.

The conversation turned to general matters for the rest of the meal. When they were ready to leave, Violet laid a hand on her friend's arm. "Think about the ranch. It would be a safe place. If nothing else, it would give you some peace of mind for a couple of months."

"I'm sure your brothers would love for a stranger to crash on them for two months."

"You're not a stranger. Plus I've kept them up to date on your success. After all, how many people have a top model for a best friend? Promise me you'll think about it."

"I will. Maybe two weeks would be okay."

"A month," Violet promptly countered.

Jessica grinned and rolled her eyes. "A month, then. I'll think about it."

Outside they hugged and said farewell. Violet hurried off to the exciting world of brain cures and research studies. Jessica put on sunglasses and a denim tennis hat that pulled down snugly around her face, then strolled through

Central Park for an hour before heading down Fifth Avenue to her home.

After nodding to a famous writer in the lobby, she walked up the steps to her floor. Although she was cordial to the man, she kept her distance. She'd learned that he'd voted against her purchasing the apartment when her approval had come before the condo association board. He didn't like celebrities in the building. He thought it contributed to strangers hanging around, hoping to catch a glimpse of the well-known person, and making a nuisance of themselves.

She wondered what the heck he thought of his own celebrity, or maybe she should say, notoriety. He had three ex-wives and a bunch of illegitimate children.

Upon letting herself in her apartment, she made sure the door locked securely behind her, then noted the blinking light on the telephone-fax-answering machine.

With a feeling of dread, she hit the play button. One message was from her boss, telling her to report in an hour early for the photo session tomorrow and to be prepared for a long day. They wanted to continue into the evening if it rained so they could get shots of lights on the wet streets and her in the latest raincoat fashions.

"Oh, thrill," she murmured.

The next four messages were silent, except for the faint hiss of breathing. On the last one, she heard the voice she recognized. "Heh…heh-heh," he chuckled, a slight pause between the start and the end of the laughter.

A shiver stormed down her spine as if she stood in the cold rain. "I hate him," she murmured as anger, resentment and fear formed a tight ball in her chest. "*Hate* him."

"Yeah?" Clyde Fortune said into the phone, which had been ringing when he walked into the house.

"Is that any way to answer the phone?" his obnoxious kid sister demanded.

"Sure. It's short and to the point."

She snorted in disapproval, then spoiled it by laughing. "How are you, my dear favorite brother?"

He grinned. "As in one of your many dear favorite brothers, according to which one you're going to ask a favor of, my sweet little sister?"

There were four boys in the family. Jack was four years older than his own thirty-six years. Since Clyde was the oldest of triplets, he had two brothers, Steven and Miles, who were the same age as he was. Violet was three years younger and the only girl among the siblings.

While the triplets had headed west when they grew up, Jack and Violet had remained in New York, where their parents lived. Their father, Patrick, was an affluent financier. Their mom, Lacey, was a feminist and an equal rights advocate. All her children had gone on marches for one cause or another during their growing years.

Clyde and his triplet brothers had loved Texas and had spent their summers on the ranch belonging to their Fortune cousins for nearly as long as they could remember. Once out of college, they'd pooled their resources and bought their own spread, the Flying Aces, two miles outside of Red Rock and not far from Ryan Fortune's Double Crown Ranch.

The brothers ran a very successful beef and egg supply business. They contracted with a major distributor in San Antonio, which was only twenty miles from Red Rock, for everything they could produce.

"I do have a favor to ask," Violet admitted.

"Uh-huh. I thought that was what you had on your little mind. Otherwise, why bother to call?"

"Don't be so cynical. Besides, the phone line runs both ways. When was the last time you called me?" she demanded.

She had a point. "Okay, I give. You're right. I haven't called in weeks—"

"Months," she corrected.

He sighed loudly. "How are our parents? Have you seen them lately?"

"I try to get out there for Sunday lunch," she told him, becoming serious. "Mom is as active as ever, but Dad is having trouble with his knees. He's slowing down."

"Well, he is seventy," Clyde said. "Tell the old man to get knee surgery. Can't you docs replace everything in the body these days, even brains?"

"Very funny," she snapped, but with humor in her tone. "I didn't call to talk about our family."

"Ah, so whose family do you want to talk about?"

"Not a whole family, just Jessica."

An image came to his mind—a tall girl with skinny arms and legs and a narrow frame, a girl who'd been shy and awkward when Violet had first brought her out to the Double Crown. The two girls had become fast friends, which he'd found surprising. Jessica had looked and sounded exactly like what she was, a down-home Texan with a twang and few social graces. Violet and the girl had remained friends all these years, had even roomed together a couple of times.

Even more surprising was the fact that Jessica was now a top model in New York, according to his sister. Since the world of fashion didn't come close to being on his list of priorities, he didn't know about that.

"Do you remember her?" Violet asked.

"Sure. Tall, awkward girl who morphed into a fashion model or something. Is that her?"

"Yes. Uh, she has a problem."

"Yeah?" He wondered what that had to do with him and the price of eggs in China or, closer to home, San Antonio.

"There's this guy, a politician who's sort of big in the city, respected family and all that." She paused.

Clyde felt tension in the back of his neck. He rubbed it away. "So?" he prodded, growing impatient.

"He's stalking Jessica."

"Call the police."

"She has. They won't do anything. There's no proof, just her word against his. Anyway, she's been working hard and this creep keeps calling and breathing into the phone, then he gives this little smirky laugh and hangs up."

Clyde muttered a curse. He didn't like people, whether men or women, who preyed on others.

"She'd planned on taking September and October off, so I thought it would be good if she got out of town."

He could sense what was coming.

"The ranch would be a perfect place for her to rest and to stay low while this jerk gets over his fixation."

"Two months? I don't—"

"She would probably only stay a month. You won't have to do a thing. She can entertain herself. She just needs a quiet place where he can't contact her."

Put that way, it was hard to refuse. "I don't know," he hedged. "Let me talk to Steven and Miles first."

"Steven doesn't even live there anymore," she protested. "He's all wrapped up in his new ranch and remodeling the house for the love of his life. And Miles won't care. He loves having a woman around to flirt with and practice his charm on. You know that."

"Huh," he said, trying to think of a good excuse not to have her friend there and knowing it was a losing battle. His protective instincts were already prodding him.

"The problem is *you*," Violet stated.

"Maybe," he conceded, wondering if the man was at fault. Maybe the model had led him on.

Once he'd been twenty-two and a gullible dreamer. He'd gone to Dallas for the annual ranchers' association meeting and fallen headlong into love with a sweet-talking waitress who'd told him she was nineteen, pregnant and abandoned by both her lover and her family. He'd given her money and set up an account for the unborn child.

Claudia had used him and his trust in her to bilk him out of a couple of thousand dollars.

He'd even proposed, thinking to bring her to the ranch and share an idyllic life. The weekend they were to marry, he'd arrived at their meeting place in Dallas and waited... and waited...and waited.

As the hours passed, he'd been in agony, worrying that she'd been in an accident or something. Yeah, right. She'd taken his money and run out on him for parts unknown. He'd also found out there had never been a child, according to her friend at the restaurant where she'd worked. The older woman had looked at him with pity.

Man, he must have had "sucker" written in big, bold letters on his forehead. Since then he'd kept his distance from women.

Ignoring the urge to dash to the rescue, he tried once more to dissuade his sibling. "Look, little sis, Jessica would be bored out of her mind staying out here."

"She wouldn't. She was born in Red Rock. She grew up there and she loves the area."

Clyde glanced heavenward. His sister was nothing if not determined once she'd set her mind on a course. "Why doesn't she stay with her family? Doesn't she have relatives somewhere around here?"

"She doesn't want to put them in danger in case the stalker follows her and gets violent. Just last month one weirdo here in New York stabbed the actress he was obsessed with. Didn't you see it in the paper?"

"I might have read something about it," he conceded. "Don't you think it's a tad strange that she won't put her family in danger but she thinks it's okay to stay with near-strangers and put their lives at risk?"

There was a tense silence on the line. "Hello?" he finally said to remind his sibling he was still there.

She cleared her throat. "I haven't exactly convinced her to head for your place. She's as stubborn as you are."

He had to laugh. "Talk about the pot calling the kettle black," he murmured.

Violet waited a second, then continued, "She doesn't want to bother anyone. She thinks it's her problem, and she has to solve it. But I'm getting worried. The guy—his name is Roy Balter—is calling more and more often. Jessica has already changed her phone number, but he got the new one."

"Info is a snap to get nowadays," Clyde said. "I've heard of this Balter guy. He was one of the talking heads on a television news program the other day. He's on the city council and is heading up a commission on terrorism. He looked okay to me."

"That's the problem. Everyone thinks he's perfectly sane, while they think Jessica is off her rocker. I was at her place last night and listened to his messages, the breathing, then this sinister little laugh. It gave me chills. Jessica is keeping the tapes from the answering machine. She says maybe the police will believe her when they find her dead body and a box of recordings from the creep."

"Damn," Clyde muttered. He closed his eyes and rubbed his neck, then gave up. "Okay, tell her she's welcome to come here next month if she wants to. I'll arrange transportation from the airport in San Antonio."

"Oh, Clyde, thank you. I don't care what other people say. I think you're absolutely wonderful." She laughed at this oft-repeated joke between them, then sobering, she said, "Would you mind picking her up? I'll feel so much better knowing she's with you. Miles is wonderful, too, of course, but he doesn't take things as seriously as you do. This may be a matter of life and death. Really."

"Yeah, yeah, I'll pick her up. Let me know the flight, date and time, okay?"

"Yes. I'll call as soon as I talk her into going. I'm sure she will. She's tired and discouraged and frustrated trying to deal with this and her work and all."

"Make sure she understands that we'll be doing the roundup while she's here. No one will have time to baby-sit or entertain her. You understand?"

"Perfectly. She just needs a break and some peace and quiet. You will keep an eye on her, won't you? I mean, in case the stalker shows up?"

He exhaled heavily. "Yes."

"Promise?"

"Promise."

With that, she said her farewells and hung up. He realized he'd forgotten to congratulate her on the article in the medical journal, which their mom had sent a couple of months ago. Not that there wouldn't be other chances in the near future. If he knew his little sis, she would hound her friend into coming out, then she would hound him about looking after the visitor.

He grabbed a beer from the fridge, which held very little else, and went out on the patio to enjoy the twilight and the cool evening air. The cattle in the two thousand acres of pasture that comprised the ranch were grazing peacefully or bedded down while they chewed their cuds.

The quiet appealed to him. No cars were on the paved county road. The interstate highway, I-35, that ran up the middle of the state through San Antonio, Austin and points north was too far away to be heard.

He liked the distance to the horizon, as if one could ride into the sunset forever. He appreciated the vastness of these wide open spaces that were so different from New York where he'd grown up.

Years ago, his mother had declared the triplets to be cowboys at heart. She said she'd known it from the moment they'd been born. Instead of crying, they'd come into the world yelling, "Whoopie-ti-yi-yo."

Or so she'd said many times with an almost perfectly straight face.

He smiled, then took a long draught of cold beer. Sometimes he missed his mom, he admitted. When she came to the ranch, she fretted about the house and its lack of a feminine touch and worried about the boys' love lives as well as their eating habits. She was into tofu and soybeans and healthy stuff. Married men, she pointed out, lived longer, healthier lives than bachelors.

She especially worried about him. When he'd returned from Dallas, alone and still single, he'd told his family his fiancée had died in a car accident and had never mentioned it again. His mother probably thought his heart was still broken.

Little did she know, as the saying went. He'd locked that unreliable organ away for good. The Flying Aces was the love of his life. It was enough.

Clyde smiled again, then frowned as he remembered his promise to his sister. Steven wouldn't care a whit if Jessica visited. Miles would flirt like mad with her when he was at the house, but most of the time he would be out on the back forty of the ranch, handling that part of the roundup.

That would leave *him* to watch after their guest.

He said a very bad word and was glad his mother wasn't there to hear it. He would have to guard his tongue if and when the visitor arrived, too.

Taking a long, long drink of the crisp, cold microbrew, he realized something else and nearly choked.

"Damn," he muttered, then gave a snort of laughter. "It figures," he said to Smoky, a dog that had drifted by last year and decided to stay, and now, attracted by the laughter, ambled over for a pat on the head.

He wondered if his sister had noted the day of the month when she'd called. That would be so like her.

It was Friday the thirteenth.

Two

The wings of the airplane dipped first one way, then the other, as the flight approached San Antonio. Jessica closed her eyes and concentrated on keeping the soda and pretzels down. She wasn't sure whether it was better to have a full stomach or an empty one when flying in bad weather.

Lightning crackled, and several people gasped. A little girl screamed. So did her mother.

St. Elmo's fire danced along the front edge of the wing. Jessica thought the fuel tanks were located in the wings. Could they catch on fire?

Summoning up her courage, she reflected on the idea of leaving New York to keep from being killed by a stalker, only to go down in an airplane crash in Texas. There was a kind of rough poetic justice in the thought.

If the plane did crash, she wouldn't have to impose on Violet's brother, who didn't want to fool with her in the first place. At least, that was the impression she'd gotten when her friend had carefully and thoroughly explained that the ranch was very busy at this time of the year.

Jessica would mostly have the house to herself and would have to find her own amusements.

Fine by her.

Clyde Fortune, the first-born of the triplets, was to pick her up. He was the least outgoing of the three. The brothers were identical triplets, all with dark hair and chocolate-brown eyes, around six feet tall, muscular bodies.

The last-born, Miles, had a dimple in one cheek, though, so maybe they weren't identical. She didn't know much about genetics, so she wasn't sure. Anyway, they looked like the proverbial peas in the pod. As a teenager, she'd had a crush on Clyde, the quiet one of the Fortune triplets.

Not that he, an older man, had known she existed.

She'd gotten over her romantic feelings quick enough when one of them had remarked that "she was so skinny and talked with such a twang, you could use her for a guitar string" when one of their friend's strings had broken.

Amusement eased the pain of that ancient insult. Her lean frame had earned her a *fortune* of her own—not in the form of a living dreamboat, but in cold cash.

At that instant, the plane touched down. Jessica thanked the heavens that they were safely on the ground. She collected her carry-on bag and all-purpose raincoat and headed for the baggage carousel.

She didn't see anyone she recognized. Several men looked her over, but none came forward. Apparently no one was waiting for her.

Wonderful, she thought, feeling like unwanted baggage. She grabbed her suitcase when it came around the moving belt, then rolled it closer to the door, not sure if her ride expected her to go outside and wait at the curb. She should have asked Violet to be more specific about what she was supposed to do.

The oddest thing happened then. Her eyes filled with tears. Astonished, she blinked rapidly until they dried up.

Thirty minutes later, she was still standing by the sliding glass doors, watching as other passengers were met by their loved ones and hugged and kissed and made to feel wanted while she wondered what to do if Clyde didn't show.

She could take a room in San Antonio under an assumed name and hide out there just as well as the Flying Aces—

"Jessica?"

She jerked around and stared into a worried face and dark eyes with a scowl in their depths. "Yes."

"Sorry to be late. There was an accident on the highway. It took thirty minutes for the police to get it cleared and let the traffic through."

"That's okay. I was just thinking of getting a room in town. Actually I could stay here just as well as at your place. It's been a long time since I've been to the Alamo."

"Violet would never let me hear the end of it if I let you do that." Clyde plucked her two cases from her. "This way."

Although he did manage to crack a smile, Jessica wasn't fooled. He was about as happy to see her as she was happy to be there. She silently said a word her mom had said she and her sister were never to use.

He led the way to his truck.

The rain hit them like bullets from the angry clouds that covered the city. She had her raincoat, which had a hood, but he wore only a light jacket. Water ran in a cascade from his gray felt cowboy hat.

His jeans were soon soaked along the entire front of the legs as the wind blew furiously against them as if trying to stop their progress. Her feet, clad in low sandals, got wet, and the cuffs of her summer slacks filled with water and wilted.

When they reached the parking space far out in the lot, he tossed her bags in the back of the crew cab pickup and her into the front. Not literally, but she had a feeling he would have liked to dispose of her as easily as the luggage.

It wasn't an auspicious start to a month-long visit, she thought.

"I'm sorry to bring you out in such weather," she said, giving him one of the brilliant smiles she was known for.

He shrugged and growled in a low tone, "We don't usually have this kind of storm in September."

Actually it was the second day of the month. A Friday. Two days ago, she'd finished the photo session and celebrated by hiding out at Violet's place so she wouldn't have to listen to the ringing of the phone every hour on the hour.

Worse—and this was what drove her into fleeing the city—was returning from her walk on Monday and finding a pale pink rose lying in the middle of her foyer. On Tuesday, a deep pink rose had been left on the sofa table. Then on Wednesday one had been placed on her pillow with all its bloodred petals torn off. Each petal had been cut in half. A police investigation had yielded no clues.

Shaken, she'd called Violet and told her friend she would love to visit the ranch for a month. They'd planned an elaborate strategy to get her packed and onto the San Antonio flight, via a separate ticket into Chicago for the first leg of the trip, with the help of a model friend.

Linda was close to Jessica in size, and had taken her place on the daily walk in the park, wearing sunglasses and a denim hat and Jessica's favorite sports outfit, just in case the stalker was watching her condo.

Glancing at her host now, Jessica wondered if it might not be worse to be trapped for a month at a remote ranch— well, two miles from town wasn't exactly remote—with a handsome but brooding Heathcliff type as her protector.

Was it better to face the evil she knew than to flee to another that she didn't? Ah, that was the question, she intoned sardonically to herself.

"Something amusing you?" Clyde asked.

She strangled the facetious smile and gave him a solemn stare. "No. I was just feeling sorry for you, being stuck with an unwanted guest for a month."

His frown could have stopped the eighteen-wheeler, coming toward them down the state highway at seventy miles an hour.

"Violet did explain that we're in the middle of roundup, didn't she?"

"Yes. You don't have to worry about entertaining me," she said graciously. The effort was wasted on him.

"Good," he said in his serious manner. "No one will have time to do any entertaining. You'll have the house to yourself during the day. I'll be in late most nights. Miles will be out in the hills and will sleep in the RV we keep for times when we can't get back to the house."

"I see. Uh, do you have a cook or housekeeper?"

"No. A woman from Red Rock comes in every Monday, to clean. Miles and I fix our own meals. Mostly eggs and toast or sandwiches," he added.

"I don't eat a lot," she quickly told him, making it clear she didn't expect him to wait on her.

His gaze ran down her like the sluice of cold rain hitting the windshield. In that one glance she felt he'd seen everything there was to see about her, both physically and mentally. It was rather daunting.

She gazed out at the land she hadn't seen in almost two years. Mmm… Yes, the last time she'd visited her folks, who lived in Austin now, had been two Christmases ago.

Her sister, brother-in-law and two nieces lived in Red Rock. They ran the hardware store Jessica had bought with her first year's earnings so her dad wouldn't lose his livelihood.

Since she figured Roy might somehow have her family watched, she was going to have to avoid them.

Also, she realized, she would have to hide in the barn or somewhere when the housekeeper arrived, in case the woman was someone who knew her or her family.

She sighed.

Her reluctant host glanced her way again.

"I'm not bored," she said as if he'd asked. She realized he probably wouldn't care if she was. "It's just that hiding out is more difficult than I'd thought it would be. I'm grateful that you're letting me stay at your place."

He hesitated, then shrugged. "It's no problem."

There was an unexpected softening in his tone that caused the ridiculous tears to burn behind her eyelids again. "Well, I know Violet twisted your arm. She can be very persistent when she gets an idea. She doesn't let go until she gets her way."

His chuckle was as pleasant as it was surprising. "Tell me about it."

"She's a wonderful friend," Jessica said. "She's always been there for me. I can still remember the first time all of you came into the hardware store with some of your cousins. I'd never seen so many Fortunes in one place before. Although I was familiar with the Texas side of the family, you New Yorkers were like exotic foreigners to me."

"I had to tell you three times what I wanted," he said.

"Ah, you remember it, too." She laughed. "I couldn't understand a word any of you said. Except Violet. She interpreted for me and glared at you and your brothers when you laughed."

"Now Steven, Miles and I speak Texan jes' like you natives," he drawled. He even smiled.

It did wonders for him, making him look younger than the thirty-six years she knew he was. His teeth were straight and very white against the tan of his face. She found herself wondering why he'd never married.

"Well," she said in mock wonder, "you have a sense of humor. Violet assured me you did, but since I was never around you guys much, I didn't believe her."

The smile disappeared. "If you're looking for charm, Miles is your man," he suggested.

"I'm not." She spoke as coolly as he had. "I'm trying to avoid one man. I'm certainly not looking to get involved with another."

Silence prevailed as he turned off the state highway onto a paved county road that led to Red Rock. Two miles before they reached the town, he turned again, this time onto the road that went past the ranch.

The road had been newly topped with asphalt and wasn't yet marked with white lines. In the darkness of the storm and the deep twilight, it seemed to disappear in the downpour. She couldn't tell where the sides of the road were or what was ahead in the rain.

He slowed to a crawl, then made the final turn onto the ranch road, which was also paved. Her heart gave an odd lurch and beat very fast. She'd never been here.

The three brothers had purchased the place after she'd moved to New York. Except for infrequent calls, she and Violet had lost touch during those years when each was getting established in her chosen career. Then Violet had returned to the city, and they had picked up their old friendship. But Jessica had never called any of the Fortunes in Texas when she returned to visit her folks.

"Oh," she said when the house came into view.

It was large and typical of the very popular Texas ranch style with a beige-painted wooden frame and shiny metal roof, a second story with a balcony over the front porch that went all the way across the front of the house and lots of shrubs and flowers in borders along the curving front walk and the dark brick foundation.

There was a four-car garage attached to the side of the house. Clyde hit the opener, then drove inside and closed the door behind them, shutting out the blowing rain.

A station wagon was the only other vehicle in the large space. There were no tools or lawn mowers. It was the neatest garage she'd ever seen.

"At our house, the one where I grew up," she clarified, "the garage was always a disaster area. My mom threatened to throw everything out on a regular basis, including the three lawn mowers. One worked. The other two didn't."

Clyde retrieved her bags and motioned toward the door into the house. She went inside.

"We use a tractor to mow the grass when we cut the hay," he said.

She followed him into a room that held a comfortable sofa and two leather recliners. A huge television was built into a bookcase-entertainment center beside a fireplace. The room led into a wide foyer that ran the length of the house.

On the other side of the foyer, she could see another room, a formal living room, although sparsely furnished.

The foyer had a graceful staircase of open oak steps and black wrought-iron railings. She could see a large dining table with six chairs beyond the steps and French doors opening onto a patio. The rain was too heavy to see what the view would be out the back of the house.

Clyde headed up the steps when she paused, not sure where to go. "This way," he said.

The foyer was repeated upstairs in a gallery-type library with bookcases and twin groupings of two chairs, a table and a reading lamp to either side. Here, too, the view through wide windows would be to the backside of the house.

"These are your quarters," he said, going into the first room on the right and flicking a light switch. A lamp on a table softly lit the room.

She glimpsed beige walls and dark furniture that was Spanish in style, plus some light oak pieces that were called Texas frontier by the local decorators.

"You have your own bath through there." He nodded toward the side of the room. "That's the closet next to it."

She also had her own private sitting space beside tall windows on the north side of the house. A large bed occupied the opposite wall.

"It looks very comfortable," she said politely.

He set her luggage on a chest at the end of the bed, then looked at her, his hands in his back pockets, his manner withdrawn. Against the dim light, his silhouette was framed against the backdrop of the bed.

A shiver ran over her while her mouth went dry. She'd learned early in New York not to mind dating men who were shorter than she was, but it was nice to go with someone she could dance with without looming over him.

Clyde Fortune fit the bill perfectly.

She saw his chest expand as he inhaled deeply. She was too tall for her head to rest against that broad expanse, but they could dance cheek to cheek.

If they ever danced.

Which she frankly doubted.

"The kitchen is downstairs," he said, striding toward the door as if he suddenly remembered an extremely important appointment that he was about to miss because of having to take care of her. "You'll find soup in the pantry, sandwich stuff in the fridge. Help yourself."

With that, he was gone.

* * *

Jessica yawned, then swung out of bed. She loved the view from the windows of her room—rolling green pastures, a thick copse of trees outlining the meandering path of a creek and then, clear skies all the way to eternity. Opening a window, she breathed deeply of the clean morning air and caught the scent of new-mown hay on the breeze.

Oh, it had been so long since she'd experienced a Texas morning! Although the humidity was high, it wasn't any worse than in the city, so that didn't bother her. Being cooped up inside did.

She hurriedly dressed in blue shorts and a matching knit top. With sneakers on her feet, she went down the steps and into the kitchen, being quiet, although she could tell by the absolute silence that she had the house to herself.

After sipping a glass of orange juice and eating one slice of unbuttered toast, she headed outside. Through an open door off the kitchen, she spotted a big pantry, plus several wall hooks. On one was a straw hat that would provide shade from the sun.

She put it on and slid the fastener up the strings and under her chin to keep the hat from blowing away in the wind. Then she headed outside to explore.

In the back, she discovered a lovely swimming pool. A small pool house, in the same style as the main one, contained a kitchen with Coke and beer in the refrigerator and microwave popcorn in the cabinet.

Okay, so she was nosy, she admitted when her conscience prodded her for snooping.

A hot tub held pride of place in the large room and an etched-glass door opened into a cedar-lined sauna with benches on three sides. There was also a full-size bathroom and next to that, surprisingly, another bedroom, making the pool house into a guesthouse, too.

"Charming," she remarked to herself, then closed the door and continued her journey of exploration.

Beyond the homestead were some barns, stables and sheds. From a velvety green field came the drone of a tractor. She spotted the huge machine but couldn't discern who was in the enclosed cab. Clyde or whoever was operating the equipment was cutting alfalfa.

Again she inhaled deeply, letting the wonderful scent flow down inside her, all the way to her roots, which sprang from the rocky Texas soil. She couldn't believe how nostalgic she'd been for home without even knowing it.

She exhaled loudly, enjoying the ambiance of the ranch. In New York, life could be so hectic…and usually was.

Here, ah, *here,* there was a sense of peace—

"Oof," she said, pitching forward against a fence post, then the ground, as something hit her on the back.

Startled, the ever-present fear of the past few months raising its ugly head, she rolled over and got a good licking in the face. Fright dissolved into laughter.

"Who are you?" she asked, sitting up while a black-and-white dog, mostly border collie, frolicked all around her.

"Smoky," a familiar voice answered.

Jessica smiled at Clyde, who'd entered the yard through a nearby gate, and leaned on her elbows while he stopped a couple of feet from her.

"Smoky, down," he ordered when the dog jumped up and planted his paws on the man. "Sit."

The dog obeyed at once.

Clyde leaned forward and offered Jessica a hand. When she clasped it, he pulled her to her feet. "Sorry about Smoky," he said in his butter-smooth baritone. "He's never met a person he didn't like."

"I like him, too." She scratched the collie's ears.

The dog rewarded her by closing his eyes and leaning into her hand in apparent ecstasy.

"You've made a slave for life," Clyde remarked. "I've got to run into Red Rock to pick up a part for the baler. Do you want to go?"

She really would have liked to ride along, but she shook her head and thanked him for the offer. "I don't think I should be seen in town. My sister and her family live in Red Rock. They don't know I'm in the area."

"Are you worried that they might be watched?"

"Yes."

A frown nicked a line across his forehead. "Maybe you shouldn't stay here alone."

"It should be okay. Roy can't possibly know where I am. Violet and I were careful to talk away from my condo and never on the phone."

A sardonic expression flickered through his eyes. "A wise precaution, I'm sure," he murmured.

Jessica realized he didn't take the threat seriously. Another thought—almost as horrifying as that of being stalked by a madman—came to her. Surely he didn't think she and Violet had planned her visit in order to...to...well, to catch his attention.

That idea had never entered her mind.

Anger bubbled in Jessica. Her friend had told her many times while they were growing up that the boys had to fight off females all the time. Huh. If *he* was conceited enough to think she was chasing him, he could think again!

"You seem to have lost your Texas twang," he said, falling into step beside her as she continued her stroll around the grounds, heading for the stables to see if they kept horses at this ranch.

"Most of it," she agreed. "I still say 'y'all' when I get excited." She kept her smile polite but remote.

"I miss it," he said suddenly.

She was certainly shocked to hear that. "I'm sure you get plenty of down-home dialect from the locals."

He nodded and smiled. "I still don't understand everything the owner at the tractor place says. His son clues me in when I look blank."

She thought of long-ago days and laughed. "The way Violet did for me when we were kids."

"Yeah."

While his tone was somewhat amused, there was a seriousness about him that didn't invite levity.

Violet had told her Clyde had been hurt by the death of his first love when he was fresh out of college and the triplets were trying to realize their dream of owning a ranch. The woman had died in an auto accident, apparently the day they were to be married.

Violet had also warned that Clyde never, ever spoke of it. For a time, Jessica had thought it was her job to ease his hurt. But she'd been young and romantic back then, she mused, excusing the impressionable girl she'd once been.

"He needs to listen to his heart again," her friend had told her gravely.

Fine. Maybe he'd meet some woman who would bowl him over and bring out those devastating smiles more often. That woman wouldn't be her, though.

"Here," he said. He held out his hand.

When she extended hers, he dropped a set of keys onto her palm. She looked at him, a question in her eyes.

"There's a station wagon in the garage. Feel free to use it. The other key is to the front door. We don't lock it, but once in a while the cleaning lady does. I don't want you to get locked out."

"Thanks. That's very thoughtful of you."

He hesitated. "If you need something at the grocery,

there's one on down the road about five miles. You don't have to go to the one in Red Rock."

"That's good. I'll get cereal and nonfat milk, if you don't mind my using the refrigerator."

"Be my guest. My mom would love to see something in it besides beer, soda, orange juice and moldy lunch meat."

He actually laughed. It was so enchanting Jessica could only gaze at him, spellbound, for a second. Then she smiled and stuck the keys in her pocket.

"See you later," she said, then snapped her fingers at the dog. "Come on, Smoky. You can be my guide while we explore the ranch." She paused and glanced at her host, who was looking at her with an unreadable expression in his eyes. "If that's okay?"

Clyde nodded. With his long, easy stride, he headed for a pickup parked next to the stable, then paused. "My parents may drop by later. Tell 'em I'll be back soon and that Miles will be here tonight. They're staying at the Double Crown this week."

"Right."

After he drove away, Jessica strolled the grounds and admired the many flowers. She assumed his parents' visit had something to do with the mysterious body found in Lake Mondo. The murder hadn't made the national news, but it had caused a big flurry of gossip and speculation in their corner of Texas. She and Violet had discussed the story at length.

The deceased man had had a birthmark on his right side, one that looked like a double crown—the same birthmark that Ryan Fortune had and that his father had named his ranch for.

Only it didn't come from the Fortune bloodline.

Ryan Fortune's father, Kingston, had been an abandoned baby, left on the doorstep of Hobart and Dora Fortune, who'd lived in Iowa. The kind and loving couple had adopted the child and raised him as their own. Kingston had grown up and moved to Texas where he became very wealthy.

The birthmark on Ryan was assumed to come from the Fortune family line, but it came from his biological grandfather, Travis Jamison. Travis had gone into the army, leaving behind a young, pregnant woman. Eliza Wise had deserted her baby and left Iowa to make a new life.

Christopher Jamison, Travis's descendent through his legitimate children and therefore cousin to Ryan Fortune, was the murdered man. He'd been a math teacher in Seattle, Washington. His fiancée seemed to think he'd come to Texas in search of his family.

Ah, well. It was none of her affair. Jessica threw her arms wide and raced down the sunny slope of the grassy lawn toward the line of trees, Smoky prancing at her heels.

There she discovered a creek running freely over a bed of sand and smooth stones. She kicked off her shoes and waded in it, feeling as buoyant as the happy child she'd once been. For the first time in weeks, she was free of worry, free of work…free, free, free!

Three

Jessica stopped at the back door. Inside she could hear the laughter of a woman, then the deeper chuckle of a man, also her host's rich baritone. She listened but couldn't detect any other voices in the house. The guests were most likely Clyde's parents.

She opened the door and felt the cooler, drier effect of conditioned air on her face. The day had gotten much warmer that the previous one, and the humidity was high. As a result, she was rather bedraggled.

After she'd explored the home area of the ranch that morning and found a lovely little lake formed by an earthen dam on the creek, she'd returned to the house and had a solitary lunch. Actually Smoky had kept her company. She'd napped, then set off exploring again in midafternoon. It was now almost six.

She quickly glanced around the pleasant kitchen. Yes, there were three people present. All eyes turned to her.

"Hello," she said, drawing on the poise learned during her years in New York. "I'm Jessica, Violet's friend. I spent a lovely weekend at your home last summer."

"And brought a lovely basket of flowers. I now use the basket on my desk to hold my mail," Lacey Fortune said, coming forward to take Jessica's arm and lead her into the room. "Patrick, you remember Jessica, don't you?"

"Yes. She beat the socks off all of us at tennis."

"It's my height," Jessica explained, shaking hands with Clyde's father. "It makes serving easier."

She'd learned to play the game as a teenager at the Double Crown Ranch when she'd gone there with Violet. She and her friend had played regularly until this year when the demands of their careers had intervened.

"I've brought food," Lacey continued, motioning toward the counter next to the refrigerator. "The boys live on air and liquids, it appears. I hope you like steak and shrimp."

"Yes." Jessica glanced at Clyde. She noticed he and his father each had a glass of the iced tea she'd made at lunch. She was thirsty, too, but first she needed a bath. "If you'll excuse me, I need to freshen up and change. Smoky and I have been exploring the ranch this afternoon."

"She likes to wade barefoot in the creek," Clyde said in a somewhat lazy, somewhat amused drawl that sent an unexpected tingle through her nerves.

"How could you know that?" she asked.

"The foreman at the egg barn heard Smoky barking and checked it out. When he spotted a strange woman romping in the creek with the dog, he called my cell number and wanted to know if I had a…"

Jessica found herself hanging on the words as Clyde paused, as if censoring the foreman's term for her.

"…a guest at the house," he finished.

Jessica frankly doubted that "guest" was the word used.

Lacey laughed and returned to putting the groceries into the proper storage bins. "Did Clinton think she was your, ahem, lady friend?" she teased with open delight, giving the younger two a speculative perusal.

Jessica felt Clyde's dark gaze drift over her in an insouciant manner that almost felt intimate. It lingered at her legs for a second before returning to her face.

"Yes," he said. He paused before asking her, "I told my parents why you're here. Do you mind?"

If he'd already explained her presence, there was hardly any point in objecting. She refrained from mentioning this obvious fact and shook her head instead.

"You and Violet both work too hard," Lacey scolded. "I've often told her to bring you out for Sunday lunch, but you rarely take a weekend off," she said.

"I'm frequently out of town or out of the country, according to what season it is," Jessica told the friendly older woman to excuse her lack of visits.

Actually she didn't want to impose on their friendship or give the impression she was a stray who couldn't make it on her own in the city. She was a big girl and she'd made her own way in the world for a long time.

"Yes, well, no wonder you needed to rest and get away from it all," Lacey said.

Jessica glanced at Clyde in confusion. He gave her a brief nod as if to say this was all he'd told his parents. She gave him a brief frown to tell him she'd appreciate being clued in on what she was to say. His answering grin was sardonic.

"Violet nagged her until she gave up and came down here," he informed his parents.

His father chuckled. "That's our daughter. She takes after her mother when it comes to noble causes…and to bossing others around and telling them what's good for them." He gave his wife a friendly tug on her hair as he teased her.

For some reason the couple's playfulness brought the stereotypical lump to Jessica's throat. She excused herself and headed up to her room.

Years ago she'd suspected that Violet's family had considered her a sort of charity case, an underdog that their daughter had taken under her cloak of compassion. The remarks confirmed this suspicion…and hurt in a way she couldn't explain.

Pride brought her head up and her chin forward as she went into her room. That same pride had made her cautious in dealing with them and was one reason she'd usually declined going to their home when Violet had tried to get her to attend family functions. It was the mother, not the daughter, who had a propensity for "causes," and Jessica had been determined not to be one.

After showering and drying her hair, she slipped into a pair of pink silk slacks with a white silk blouse printed with pink flowers. A pink stretchy band held her hair away from her face, leaving it free to flow down her back in a nearly straight, shimmering cascade that was part of her casual hometown-girl persona the photographers loved.

She brushed bronze highlights onto her cheeks and a coral pink color onto her lips. A couple of flicks with the mascara wand brought out the length of her eyelashes and the robin's-egg-blue of her eyes. She pulled on the black ballerina slippers she liked to wear around the house and returned downstairs.

Clyde was in the kitchen, chopping vegetables.

"May I help?" she asked.

"You want to finish the salad?"

"Sure. Are all these to go in it?" She indicated the vegetables on the counter beside the sink.

"Yes. Mom's a stickler for lots of veggies. Don't chop them too fine. She likes to be able to identify what she's eating, she says."

"Right. Uh, about my being here," she said, lowering her voice to a near whisper as she came close to him. "Was that all you told your parents—that I was here for a rest?"

"Yes." His gaze was cool when he glanced at her. "She would worry if she thought one of her chicks was in danger. That includes you, I'm afraid."

"Me? Why?"

He gave a sardonic snort. "How long have you and Violet been friends?"

"Since we were twelve."

"That's twenty-one years. With you both being in New York, that friendship has grown. Mom considers you one of hers now."

"Oh." She had to laugh.

"What?" He handed her the paring knife and observed while she sliced carrots into the huge salad bowl.

"When I was a kid I saw a cartoon about a city mouse that visited his mouse cousin who lived on a farm. I've always wondered if your family thought I was a country mouse that Violet befriended. I think you just answered that."

"You've traveled far from your roots, Texas gal," he said in a tone that was husky and, while not exactly harsh, held an undercurrent of accusation, as if she'd done something that personally offended him.

She was intensely aware of his gaze as it studied her face, swept down her body, then came back to her face and locked on her mouth before meeting her eyes.

"I was lucky," she said. "A fortuitous lineup of the stars that led to success."

"Not to mention a gorgeous face and the lean, taut body prized by the fashion industry."

Now he sounded merely ironic, she noted, but still her nerves did their tingly thing. "Actually, I'm not gorgeous," she corrected, her own voice low and soft, deliberately sexy. "Sondra says I'm 'striking,' which is better than mere beauty because it lasts forever."

"Sondra being…?"

"My agent."

"Ah, yes. I recall your father worrying when you first went to New York. He said you lived with an older woman, but the woman was divorced, so he and your mother weren't sure she was a good example."

Jessica gave him a surprised stare. "You talked to my parents about me?"

He shrugged. "Red Rock is a small town, and we did business at the hardware store. You were frequently the subject of conversation by the locals."

She nodded and went back to chopping veggies. "People seem to have a proprietary interest when a hometown girl, or guy, makes good. It was nice to come home and know they were proud of me. However, it was Sondra who made most of the decisions early on in my career, and my dad who advised me on saving my earnings. They're the ones who guided me."

"But you're the one who put in the hours of work," he reminded her. "In the store your father displayed pictures of you at your first job. I have to admit I wouldn't have recognized you. You looked very different from the long-legged teenager I remembered."

Jessica felt heat skim her cheeks. She hoped he didn't also remember that, at nineteen, she'd had a terrible crush on him. She'd wanted to make him notice her.

Looking into his eyes, she suddenly understood the dark moodiness in those depths. He, Clyde Fortune of the famous Fortune family, was attracted to her.

Instead of feeling elated, she was disappointed. He was attracted to the persona developed by her career—the casual, laughing and oh-so-sexy summer blonde who was poised, outdoorsy and cosmopolitan.

That was the way the fashion photographers saw her and what they picked up in the photo sessions. It was the persona she and Sondra had decided to cultivate long ago, but whether in New York, Paris or Milan, she knew, at heart, she was simply a Texas gal a long way from home.

She focused her attention on the task at hand and away from the banked embers of interest that resided in his gaze. It needed only a spark between them to set the flames to a fiery glow. She wouldn't provide that spark.

He headed for the door. "I'd better get the grill started so we can eat. Miles should be in soon. The folks are staying at the Double Crown, so they won't be spending the night."

"Are they here for the funeral?"

He frowned. "What do you know about that?"

"Violet explained the connection to Ryan Fortune. It was also in the San Antonio paper. My sister read it and called me."

"Did she also relate the local gossip?"

Jessica shook her head. She and her sister had speculated on the dead man's relationship to the mighty Fortunes of Texas, but she wasn't sure what gossip Clyde referred to.

"Some people think Ryan might have murdered Christopher Jamison to keep his father's true origins a secret."

Jessica was shocked at the idea. "No one knowing Ryan Fortune would believe that."

"No?" Clyde questioned. "Then you don't know your fellow Texans as well as I assumed you did."

With that, he left. She continued preparing the salad. When she finished, she stored the stuff in the refrigerator, which was now filled with all kinds of healthful food, including nonfat milk and yogurt, two of her usual food staples.

After pouring a glass of iced tea, she went outside. She found Clyde on the other side of the pool/guesthouse at a built-in grill.

"Well, what have we here?" an appreciative male voice inquired. "Ah, yes, the fair Jessica." Miles, the youngest of the triplets, looked her over. "Very fair indeed. The duckling has changed into the swan, brother. You didn't mention that when you reported she'd arrived."

"Hello, Miles," she said, holding out her hand.

Instead of shaking it, Miles tucked her hand into the crook of his arm and led her to a table under an arbor covered with rose vines. He held a chair for her, then took the one beside it.

"So start at the beginning and tell me of your life in the big city," he invited. He took a drink of beer and gazed at her in open admiration.

Jessica was used to this kind of attention, so it didn't rattle her at all, unlike the black scowl she was getting from Clyde. She tried to figure out if she'd done something wrong. Nothing came to mind.

"Both Violet and I have been busy," she began. "We try to meet for lunch at least once a week."

From the side of the house came the tinkling laughter of his mother. Patrick and Lacey joined them on the patio. She held a posy of late summer blossoms in her hand.

"A centerpiece for the table," she said. "Miles, come help me find a vase for them. Are we going to eat out here or in the house?" she asked Clyde.

"In the house. We've had a new hatch of mosquitoes since the storm."

Lacey smiled at Jessica. "They leave terrible itchy bumps on me, but never seem to bite the men."

"That hardly seems fair," Jessica murmured, wishing a swarm would descend on Clyde. What the heck had she done to tick him off?

"The steaks will be ready in ten minutes," he said. "Miles, if you'll bring the shrimp when you come back out, I'll put them on."

When the other three went inside, Jessica surveyed the grounds and didn't glance at Clyde, who now wore dark slacks and a white shirt with the sleeves rolled up on his arms.

"Miles, you might recall, is something of a tease," Clyde said without preamble. He gave her a stern glance.

"Yes? Is there a message for me in that statement?"

"Don't get your hopes up that it means anything when he flirts with you."

She did a slow burn. "Actually," she murmured wickedly, "I have my hopes centered on you."

He choked on his beer.

Smiling, she took a long, cool drink of iced tea.

"I really don't see why I have to come along," Jessica said on Sunday afternoon.

"So I can keep an eye on you," Clyde answered.

"No one knows where I am. Except your family," she added. "Now everyone will."

"The people in Hanson Park probably won't recognize you," he said calmly. "Keep your sunglasses on and the hat pulled low."

She felt like a latter-day Mata Hari, on a mission and trying to keep up a pretense of disguise. Clyde had insisted she attend the funeral of Christopher Jamison rather than stay at the ranch alone all afternoon and evening. It would be very late before they returned home, he'd said.

His parents would be with Ryan Fortune and his wife, Lily. Miles was coming in his own truck. She and Clyde were in the station wagon, which was clean and more comfortable for the trip than the pickup, he'd told her.

She didn't recall his being so bossy years ago.

After flicking a piece of lint off the navy blue pants suit, she sighed, settled into the seat and gazed at the landscape, a cloud of depression hovering over her. Funerals were hardly joyous occasions.

Unfortunately, where the rich and famous congregated, the press also made an appearance.

"I told you I shouldn't have come," she muttered.

"The police will keep the reporters at bay," Clyde said, driving through an ornate wrought-iron gate to a private parking area after an officer had checked his identity and waved them through.

Two reporters pushed forward, but they were ordered back behind the police barriers that cordoned off the lane leading to the church and cemetery.

When she and Clyde got out of the station wagon, Jessica kept her wide-brimmed lacy hat on, effectively covering her hair, which she'd twisted up on the back of her head. Very dark sunglasses hid her trademark blue eyes.

The funeral chapel was filled to overflowing. The entire Fortune family was there, it seemed. Jessica recognized most of those from Texas. Ryan's twin daughters, Vanessa and Victoria, were present with their husbands.

Jessica nodded to them, then to Lily, Ryan's wife. His third wife, she recounted. Apparently they'd been in love long ago, but fate had intervened. Now they were together again and very happy in their marriage, according to Violet.

Clyde made sure she stayed close to him, as if he'd put a claim in on her. Whenever his suit sleeve brushed her arm, shimmering tingles flowed through her like champagne bubbles dancing through her blood. It was disconcerting to be so aware of another person.

The last time she'd felt so utterly alive, she'd been nineteen and in the throes of her first great love.

With him.

"Clyde, Jessica, this is Blake and Darcy Jamison," Lacey introduced the parents of the deceased young man. "You've already met Clyde. Jessica is a longtime friend of our daughter, Violet."

"How do you do?" she said politely. "I'm terribly sorry for your loss."

She really was. She couldn't imagine a worse pain than losing a child. Violet had told her of the death of a patient and the woman's unborn child just before Jessica left New York. It had been a terrible case, and the family had blamed Violet and the neurosurgeon who'd performed the risky surgery for the tragedy.

The Jamisons' son had been a handsome young man in his prime and a respected teacher. It was sad.

"This is our youngest son, Emmett," Mr. Jamison said.

Emmett Jamison was around Clyde's height and had the muscular build of someone who stayed in shape. He had short dark hair and attractive green eyes that seemed to take in everything going on around him without overtly noticing anything in particular. From the slump of his shoulders, he seemed overwhelmed by the death of his older brother.

During dinner the previous evening, Jessica had heard Lacey mention that Emmett was with some government agency now, but he'd once had a career as a legal advisor on Wall Street.

An interesting career change. She wondered what had prompted it.

There was also another Jamison brother, according to Lacey, one who was estranged from the family and hadn't been seen in a long time. Jessica couldn't imagine deliberately cutting herself off from her parents, sister, a very nice brother-in-law and two adorable nieces.

At least a dozen reporters stood at the fence to the Hanson Park cemetery and jotted down notes as the silent group gathered inside the lovely grounds for the last ritual of the service.

Jessica noticed eyes on her—it was impossible to disguise her height although she wore flats—and the photographers who snapped pictures of everyone who passed through the gate. She hid behind Clyde's greater bulk as much as possible in an attempt to keep her identity unknown.

He took her arm at one point as they crossed the grass. From the glances of the Jamisons' friends, she was sure they thought she was with the handsome rancher as more than a friend of the family.

As she observed the Fortune and Jamison families, she saw that Ryan, now patriarch of the Texas Fortunes, and Patrick, of the New York Fortunes, and Blake Jamison seemed to have formed a close friendship.

From their mingled heritage—with Ryan being kin to Blake by blood and to Patrick by adoption—the three men probably had a lot to discuss concerning their family connections. It was puzzling that Blake's son, who was from Seattle, should have been found murdered and left in a lake near Ryan's ranch in Texas.

After the funeral, those connected by family ties returned to the Jamison home. Jessica quietly positioned herself in a side chair almost hidden by a palm tree and wished they would soon leave for the ranch. It was getting dark and the trip was lengthy.

A buffet dinner was ready for the mourners, and the guests talked quietly of happier times. Darcy Jamison related some mischief her three sons had gotten into when they were very young boys.

Clyde's mom had earlier told similar tales about her five children. Jessica especially liked the one about the triplets' lemonade stand that had been so successful they'd caused a traffic jam and neighbors had called the police on them.

A while later, while Jessica sipped an iced tea, alone, she overheard Clyde's smooth baritone. "I'm going to collect Jessica and head back to the ranch," he said.

Jessica was relieved to hear this news.

"Good," his mother replied. "Try to be pleasant to her."

"What's that supposed to mean?" His voice was polite but carried a note of irritation.

"I mean," said his mother, "that you ignore your guest to the point of rudeness. Your father and I noticed it last night at dinner. Then you glared at Miles when he talked to Jessica. You did the same thing when Emmett Jamison spoke to her earlier today. Jealousy isn't a becoming trait."

"I'm hardly jealous," he scoffed in a cool tone.

Lacey wasn't daunted. "Well, you act like it."

"I'm keeping an eye on her—"

Jessica silently groaned as he stopped abruptly.

"Why?" his mom immediately asked.

His sigh was audible. "She had some problem with a guy in New York hounding her for a date. That's why Violet talked her into hiding out at the ranch. No one is supposed to know where she is. I would appreciate it if you would keep this information to yourself, okay?"

"Of course," Lacey said in a very interested manner. "So you're protecting her?"

"At Violet's insistence," he admitted.

"Good," she said. "I'm proud of you for helping out. But try to be a bit more cordial to Jessica, won't you? Even if she is an unwanted burden you've taken on."

Jessica's ears burned at this last assessment, but she'd known it was true from the beginning. She'd never wanted others to know and feel sorry for her. That was why she was angry and embarrassed.

Slipping from the chair, she went the long way around the room and approached Clyde and Lacey from a different direction so they wouldn't suspect she'd overheard their conversation. She smiled as cordially as she could.

"Ready to go?" he asked.

She nodded and bid his mother goodbye.

While Clyde went to say his farewells to his father and Mr. and Mrs. Jamison—Emmett had already gone—Lacey laid a hand on Jessica's arm. "Clyde was engaged when he was twenty-two. Sadly she died. He's slow to open up, but once he gives his loyalty to someone, he's a friend forever."

"How admirable," Jessica murmured, keeping her tone neutral. "It was wonderful seeing you and your husband again. Give my regards to Violet when you see her."

"Didn't she tell you?" Lacey asked in surprise. "She went on a cruise and will be gone for a couple of weeks."

"She's mentioned getting away before, but I didn't realize she'd already gone."

"It was very sudden," Lacey confided.

"There was a case…the mother and child died. It upset Violet very much," Jessica told the other woman. "I was worried about her and tried to get her to come to the ranch with me. I think she needs some time alone."

Lacey nodded, but worry still lurked in her eyes. "At least Steven is settled with someone he loves. They're getting married soon. Did Clyde tell you?"

"No, but Violet did," Jessica said. "I understand his fiancée has been helping the governor plan charity events. That puts Steven into some pretty lofty circles here in Texas."

"As long as they love each other, I don't care if Amy plans shows for prize pigs."

Jessica laughed with the other woman. She liked Clyde's parents. They had never been pretentious or uppity about their wealth and social position.

"Ready to go?" Clyde asked, returning to the two women.

His mother kissed his cheek, then did the same to Jessica. "Be careful on the road," she cautioned in the manner of mothers everywhere.

"I'm always careful," he said with a rather rakish grin, then he turned to Jessica. "Let's hit the road before some other male makes a beeline for you."

In the station wagon, she buckled up and waited until they were on the road. "It's because I'm so sweet," she said.

"What?" He gave her a puzzled glare.

She flashed him her sweetest smile. "That's why I attract so many admirers. Because I'm so sweet."

"Huh," he snorted.

She smiled and slid deeper into the seat to enjoy the silent ride back to Red Rock and the Flying Aces spread. Not having grown up with brothers, she hadn't realized how gratifying it was to annoy the heck out of an arrogant male.

Four

A drizzle began to fall on the return trip. Clyde glanced at Jessica, silhouetted by the blackness of the night and dimly illuminated by the dashboard lights. The rain wouldn't do that silky outfit any good.

"Wait," he said when they arrived at the ranch. "I think there's an umbrella in the car."

He fished the old umbrella out of the back of the station wagon and held it over Jessica's head when he opened the door for her. He'd parked as close to the porch as possible so she wouldn't get wet.

There, that ought to prove to his mom that he was considerate.

He frowned as he opened the front door and flicked on the lights inside, brightening up the length of the foyer with wall sconces and a lamp in the living room.

The air inside the house felt cold compared to the

muggy ambiance outside. He saw Jessica shiver and wrap her arms across her middle.

"How about a cup of hot chocolate?" he asked, putting on a jovial air.

"You don't have to be nice to me," she told him, giving him one of those dead-level stares she was so good at.

Since she was nearly his height, it was effective. With other men, it must be damned intimidating to be so calmly and unemotionally looked down on by a beautiful woman.

Correction—a striking woman.

Either way, she attracted a man's eye. It hadn't even occurred to him that she would arouse all his primitive instincts when he'd okayed her visit. However, he'd been expecting his kid sister's friend, not this…this…poised, silky smooth, graceful *female*.

"Yes, I do have to be nice to you, or else my mother will pin my ears back," he said, tossing his suit jacket and tie on the nearest dining room chair and heading into the kitchen.

Jessica, he noted, had stopped by the stairs.

"Why don't you change out of those damp clothes while I make the hot chocolate?" He managed to speak in a casual tone, but blood pumped hard through his lower regions at the images that sprang into his mind.

He could imagine those long slender legs tangled with his, wrapped around his hips, straddling his body….

"All right." She disappeared up the stairs.

By concentrating on the task, he got the warm drink made without spilling milk and cocoa all over the counter, but it wasn't easy. His hands were actually trembling.

He muttered a word he couldn't use in polite company.

"I beg your pardon?" Jessica entered the kitchen and gave him a questioning look.

"Nothing." He forced his eyes to stay on the cups he carried to the island counter. But part of his mind had already taken in the long blue nightgown that peeked out from the lacy blue robe with each step she took. The color was a knockout with those blue eyes of hers.

She slid onto one of the three stools and took a sip of the cocoa and declared it "delicious."

He sat down, keeping one stool between them, and tried to think of something pleasant to say.

"The rain is getting heavier, and the wind seems to be picking up," she remarked, her eyes on the windows. "It was raining Friday, too, when you picked me up."

"It's that time of year," he said inanely.

"Yes, June to November. Thunderstorms and hurricanes. I remember." She paused, then asked, "What's wrong?"

He shrugged, irritated and frustrated with his barely controlled libido. "With the ranch? Nothing. With life? Who knows?"

"I think it's something to do with the funeral, or rather, with the death of Christopher Jamison."

"The *murder* of Christopher Jamison," he corrected, hearing the harshness in his voice.

"Do you know something about it?"

He gazed into her eyes and saw only sympathy. So she wasn't asking out of morbid curiosity. He frowned as some part of him softened fractionally. "I've got bad vibes about it. Nothing specific, but a feeling…."

He tried to find words to describe the vague uneasiness that wouldn't let up. It was impossible.

"He was young and healthy," he finally said. "He fought with his attacker, according to the rumor, but…I don't know. Something doesn't feel right."

"Maybe whoever it was took him by surprise."

"Maybe. But what was he doing at the lake by himself?"

"Fishing?" she suggested. "Thinking about life? His fiancée said she thought he was looking for someone."

Clyde heaved a frustrated sigh. "The police don't seem to be doing much."

"I'm sure there are things going on that we don't know about. Ryan Fortune isn't going to let the murder pass without trying to find out who, what, why and all that."

"Yeah? I suppose you charmed information out of Ryan at the funeral?" He regretted the sarcasm immediately and opened his mouth to apologize.

She spoke first. "His wife Lily said their housekeeper saw a red ring around the moon a few months ago. That means trouble, usually death. I know how it feels to be bothered by something you can't quite define, especially when it indicates danger or a tragedy you can't quite grasp."

Clyde noticed Jessica's fingers trembled as she lifted the cup to her lips. She wore no lipstick now, but her lips were a pale pink, very soft-looking...very enticing.

He stared while she drank then licked the foam off her upper lip, the motion as delicate as a cat swiping cream off its whiskers. He licked his own lips and thought of things he could be doing to her, with her.

His blood hit fast boil. Sweat broke out on his brow. His body went rigid while his control shredded. He resorted to a sneer of amusement, knowing it was underhanded. It was the only thing he had left as a defense.

"Superstition, Texas gal," he scoffed. "After your years in the city, you should be past your country upbringing, shouldn't you?"

Her eyes flicked to him. There was intelligence as well as fury in those bright blue depths. "I don't think so," she drawled in a slow, provocative manner. "My country instincts have served me rather well in the city."

"Yeah? Like how?"

"Like knowing when a man is interested because I'm a model and he thinks that means I sleep around. I don't," she said flatly, her eyes sweeping over him as if she could see every sizzling pulse point in his body.

Clyde felt the heat rush to his head. Okay, he'd asked for that one. An apology was definitely in order.

"I'm sorry," he began.

"Oh, don't bother," she snapped, frowning as she took another drink and licked those delectable lips again.

He went into meltdown. Again. He cleared his throat. "You don't cut a fellow much slack," he said in a carefully amiable voice.

She gave him a glance that could have sliced bread without leaving a crumb. "I heard your mother."

He tried to figure out if this was a trick. Women were good at turning the tables on a man and making him feel guilty for something he didn't even think of doing.

"What about my mother?" he asked cautiously.

Again the laser glance, then a sarcastic half laugh. "She told you to be cordial to me. After all, I am a guest in your house, albeit an unwelcome one."

She appeared cool, poised and aloof. Yet he sensed, in some way he didn't comprehend, that he'd hurt her, and he was truly sorry for that.

"You're not unwelcome," he told her, peering straight into her eyes so she could see he meant what he said. "But you are a surprise. You left Texas shortly before I returned here to live. Sometime in those years between then and now, you changed from a cygnet into a swan, from a girl into a woman." He managed a smile. "Be careful, or I'll be tempted to show you how pleasant I can be to a guest."

One eyebrow rose, mocking him. "Oh, yeah?"

"Yeah."

He tried to suppress the urge to answer the challenge in her frank appraisal. Her gaze ran over him, paused at the ridge behind his zipper, then returned to his face.

His pulse leaped at the expression in those blue depths. Gone was the challenge, the sardonic edge. In its place was an intimate darkness, a timeless hunger that he recognized at once.

"Jessica," he said, the word filled with warning and a yearning he hadn't even realized he had.

When she licked her lips again and swallowed as if it was difficult to do, he was lost.

Without another thought, he removed the mug from her hand and pushed it, with his, to the far side of the counter. Then he reached for her.

Her lips were warm and as soft as he'd known they would be. There was a surprising hesitation in her response, something like shyness…or a wildness she held under a tight control.

He didn't want control or shyness, he found. He wanted a wild, explosive need that matched the one raging through his blood like hot quicksilver.

"Jessica," he said on a low groan, standing and pulling her up so their bodies fit together as perfectly as two interlocking pieces carved from one branch.

She was all soft, silky warmth in his hands. He rubbed his palms over her back, her hips.

"You remind me of a birch sprout," he told her, encircling her waist with his hands, "so lean and supple in my hands I feel as if I should shape you into something special, something sensuous and delicate, yet strong and beautiful."

"Your own Pygmalion?"

She smiled into his eyes. The lambent gleam dipped right down inside him. "You make me want to do things I haven't thought about in a long time."

She slid her hands up his arms, then laid them on his shoulders, her fingers caressing him through his shirt and sending fireballs along his flesh. "Such as?" she asked, leaning her head back a bit so she could gaze at him.

"Forget work and responsibility." He kissed her throat, finding the pulse that beat with a rapid flutter beneath her wonderfully soft skin. He licked the spot, then sucked lightly as if he thought of biting her at that vulnerable point. "Forget everything except the pleasure to be found in this." He kissed down the center line between her breasts. "And this."

With his lips, he caressed the tip of her breast and felt it tighten through the thin fabric of the gown and robe. He wanted her naked and in his arms. Now.

"I want to undress you, very slowly…very, very slowly," he continued, "and explore all the hidden treasures I know are waiting under this blue froth of lace and silk, waiting just for me."

He felt a shiver run over her, then the gentle sway of her body against his, driving his lust like wind driving a storm ashore to wreak what havoc it could. They were both in danger of being swept away. And, God help him, he wanted to ride that wave of temptation and danger.

Moving one step, he meshed their thighs, then had to grit his teeth as need became almost painful. He heard her sharply inhaled breath and knew it was the same for her.

Unable to resist, he kissed her deeply, thoroughly, endlessly. When they were both breathless and unsteady on their feet, he forced himself to take one step back from the brink of the fiery abyss where they stood.

"I could make love to you right here," he said in a hoarse murmur. "Standing right here, pressed up against the counter and not caring who walked in and found us."

She opened her eyes and blinked up at him, so sexy, so lost to passion, that he nearly kissed her again.

"And you wouldn't stop me," he said softly. "You're as deep into this as I am."

"I know," she whispered, the fires they'd ignited still dancing in her eyes. "It's madness."

"But it would be good, so good between us, that the thought drives the sane intentions right out of my head. All I can think about is touching you. I want to see you. I need it, more than air, I think."

Although he wondered what the heck he was doing, he proceeded to push the lacy robe off her shoulders, then slip the straps of the nightgown down her arms.

The material caught on the provocative tips, then slipped free and pooled at her waist. He stared at the tender buds waiting for his caress. He let the anticipation build, enjoying the visual pleasure to the full.

When she moaned and tightened her clasp on his shoulders, he chuckled and bent forward until he found the treat. He nibbled and licked at each breast with great care.

No one, he thought, searching past the rosy haze that enveloped them both, had ever pleased him more, had ever excited him to this pitch. It was overpowering, mind-blowing. *Dangerous.*

He pulled back just before all thought disappeared entirely, before he was sucked into passion so hard and wild and shattering, he would never recover. What was he doing? He desperately needed to regain control over himself.

He raked a hand through his hair and let out a ragged breath.

"Party's over, gal," he managed to drawl. "Go to bed before I forget my promise to my sister."

He watched the haze clear from her eyes and regretted its loss.

"What promise?" she asked.

"To protect you." He sighed heavily. "I think that includes from myself. Especially myself." He headed for the back door while he could still force his legs to walk.

Miles was in the kitchen when Jessica entered the next morning. "It's safe," he told her with a dazzling smile. "Grumpy bear has left to separate the calves to be sold from the rest of the herd."

"He's grumpy this morning?" she asked with wide-eyed innocence. "How unusual."

They laughed at their joke, and that was the moment Clyde walked into the kitchen and over to the sink. He held a handkerchief around his left index finger.

"What happened?" Miles asked while Clyde washed his hands under the running water.

"Some stupid cattle broke through the fence just below the dam. One of them had a piece of barbed wire around its neck. I got cut while removing it."

"You need me to stay here today and repair the fence?"

Clyde shook his head. "I've got a temporary fix on it. The trucks will be here early this afternoon. After they leave, I'll string new fencing."

"Okay. Well, I'm off for the back forty." Miles stood, yawned and stretched, shook his head and started for the back door. "See ya in about three days," he said to Jessica, then was gone.

After the sounds of Miles's pickup faded, the room echoed with silence.

Jessica got out an egg and one piece of toast.

"Is that all you eat?" Clyde finally said, now holding a paper towel around his injured finger. At her nod, he muttered, "No wonder you stay so skinny."

"I'm not skinny," she corrected coolly. "My weight is just right for my bone structure."

"Huh."

She made a face at his back. "Do you want some breakfast? I'm going to scramble an egg with cheese."

He hesitated, then nodded.

When he gave a low curse, Jessica sighed, but bravely went over to see what was the problem. He was having trouble getting a bandage on his finger, she saw.

"Here, let me." She removed a square of gauze from the first-aid kit, folded it into fourths, then held it in place over the wound to help stop the bleeding while she dried his hand with another paper towel. She wrapped the end of his finger with tape, securing the gauze in place tightly. "There, that should do it. Keep your hand above your heart for a few minutes to help stop the bleeding."

"I suppose you've had medical training," he said.

She broke four eggs into a bowl and, with a fork, beat them as hard as she could. Upon realizing what she was doing, she eased up. "Don't subject me to your waspish humor this morning," she told him. "Last night wasn't my fault."

"Whose the hell was it?" he asked with a snarl and a black scowl in her direction.

She popped three pieces of toast into the toaster slots. "Yours."

A muscle in his strong jaw flexed a couple of times.

She relented. "Well, both of ours, I suppose."

"But I made the first move."

A major concession. She smiled slightly. "It was something we both wanted. I had a terrible crush on you years ago, you know. I once heard a couple of local girls at Emma's Café discussing the Fortune triplets' kissing technique. I was jealous that I'd never experienced it for myself. Now I have."

He loomed very close all of a sudden. "And?"

She studied his expression as she poured the eggs into

the hot skillet. "Pretty devastating. I'd rate you a nine and a half."

"Why not a ten?" he demanded.

She rolled her eyes at this show of male arrogance. "Because you regretted it afterward. Because you acted as if the whole situation was my fault. Because you're acting like a bone-headed mule this morning. I had to take off a half point for attitude."

That seemed to set him back on his heels. She let him simmer while she finished preparing their meal. While they ate, he kept tossing little scowls her way as if he really wanted to say something nasty to her, but couldn't decide if he should or not. She hid her laughter and gave him several bland smiles each time she caught his eye.

"That was very good," he said politely when he finished. He put his plate in the dishwasher, then poured coffee in an insulated travel mug. "I'll probably be working late today. I won't be in for lunch."

He left by the back door, and she watched his progress across the yard to the barn, his long legs making quick work of the distance. He loaded strands of fencing and the tools he would need, then drove off after telling Smoky to stay at the house when the dog started to leap into the truck.

Jessica cleaned the kitchen, got her book and went to the creek to hide. Today was Monday and the housekeeper was due. Smoky joined her and flopped down in the shade beside her with a loud sigh. She scratched his ears and proceeded to read.

At six, Jessica peered out the back windows and wondered when her host was going to call it a day. She could see the front bumper of his truck gleaming in the late afternoon sun where it was parked among the trees next to the creek.

Earlier, big trucks had arrived and Clyde had directed the loading of the cattle that would go to auction. That had taken over two hours. He'd worked through lunch, then headed for the creek below the dam to repair the fence. He'd been there for the remainder of the day.

Restless, she looked in the fully stocked refrigerator and spotted some deli-sliced roast beef, whole-wheat buns with sesame seeds on top and kosher dill pickles. Her favorite.

On an impulse, she made up three sandwiches, put pickles and chips in plastic bags and used a decorative basket on top of the fridge to carry the food. She added two cans of soda and two straws.

Slipping on comfortable clogs, she whistled for Smoky and the two of them strolled down to the creek, following the path past the dam and to the section where the creek made a sharp turn around a stand of trees. She didn't see anyone working on the fence.

Smoky startled a rabbit and the two set off in a run across the pasture. Several cows stared after them as if wondering what all the fuss was about.

"Clyde?" she called, stopping at the higher elevation next to the dam. Several feet below that point she could see the shiny new section of fence attached to two new posts. The hair stood up on her neck at the lack of sound or the presence of the man.

The sound of splashing water caused her to jerk. She whirled in time to see broad shoulders emerge from the depths of the small lake. Her host stood and shook his head, sending water in a rainbow spray about his muscular body.

She realized he was nude.

The water level reached the midpoint of his hips. Below that, she could clearly discern the taut outline of his thighs. At her gasp, he turned abruptly.

They stared at each other, frozen in time and place for

an eternity. His chest rose as he took a deep breath, then sank into the water up to his neck.

"Good timing," he said, his smile as challenging as it was unfriendly. Well, not exactly unfriendly...

She indicated the basket. "You missed lunch. I thought you might enjoy a picnic."

"Yeah, I would."

But his eyes told her his mind wasn't on food.

Neither was hers. She felt as if she'd been sucked into a blast furnace as heat spread all over her, through her and down her bare legs, where his gaze was now taking a leisurely inventory. He took in her tummy, visible between the white shorts and the red knit crop top.

"I'm coming out," he said.

A warning she didn't heed. They perused each other as the distance between them closed. She noted the movement of his muscles, the breadth of his shoulders, the smooth tan to a point just below his waist, then the pale strip of skin from there to his legs, which, like hers, were tan from wearing shorts.

She swallowed, her breath coming out harshly as her lips parted to admit more air. He was undeniably male. *Aroused* male.

The picnic basket slipped from her numb fingers and brushed the side of her foot as it hit the ground.

Then he was there, directly in front of her. He stared into her eyes for five seconds, then his big hand closed around the back of her head and brought her into the kiss.

She stepped forward and his wet body was plastered against her, soaking her shorts and top with coolness, then warmth, incredible warmth.

He made a sound deep in his throat, a groan that echoed the need raging through her. She clung to him in shameless hunger.

"Jessica?" he questioned.

"Yes," she whispered. "Yes, yes, yes."

He swung her up into his powerful embrace and walked down the incline to a sandy spot in the shade of the trees. He set her down and murmured, "Wait."

She watched as he retrieved a tarp and a long towel from the pickup. These he spread over the sandy bed, then held out a hand to her. She went to him without hesitation.

When he dropped to his knees on the makeshift pallet, she did, too. He ran his fingertips along her cheeks, then down her neck to her breasts. He cupped each one in his palms and brushed the tight nipples with his thumbs.

With a low sound, he pulled her into his arms. She closed her eyes and gave herself to the kiss and the moment, knowing there would be no going back.

Clyde felt the sweet yielding as Jessica leaned into him, not caring that he'd gotten her wet. "I've got to have more," he whispered. "I have to see you, feel you."

When he hooked his fingers on the damp material of her top, she lifted her arms and let him pull it over her head. He tossed it onto a tree branch, then followed it with the white lace-trimmed bra. When he nudged her backward, she lay on the towel and helped him slip the rest of her clothing away from her smooth, slender body.

He let his gaze move slowly over her, from one perfect point to another, taking in the shape and curve and texture of her. "One more thing," he said.

He removed the band from her hair, laid it on the clogs she'd left beside the tarp and ran his fingers along the glossy locks so that it covered her breasts. The pink nipples peeked between the honey-golden strands in an impudent way that made him smile.

"You're right," he said. "You're not skinny. You're

beautiful. Beautiful," he repeated firmly as if she'd argued with him.

When she smiled up at him, his heart stopped, just stopped.

"Come to me," she said. "Now!"

Jessica heard the entreaty in her voice and wondered if she was giving too much away. Her innermost feelings churned in a whirling ball of uncertainty and longing. She wanted this moment more than she'd ever wanted anything.

"Whatever tomorrow brings," she murmured.

"Forget tomorrow," he said with a smile but a serious undertone.

Lifting her arms, she urged him close and sought his lips for another of the spellbinding kisses that taunted her heart with things that would never be.

He explored every inch of her, making her aware of sensitive places she'd never encountered before. She did the same to him, touching him as she'd once wanted to all those many years ago when she'd been nineteen and in love.

As her hands moved slowly down his hips and then became more intimate, Clyde grasped at control, determined to make the moments last. But he was near the exploding point.

So was she. It pleased him deeply to know she was moist and ready for him, that she wanted him as much as he wanted her. The intensity of her gaze almost did him in when she opened those lovely blue eyes and followed the path of her hands over his taut body.

"You're making me crazy," he warned.

He both heard and felt her soft laughter. "Good," she said. "That's what you're doing to me."

When she prodded, he shifted his weight over her. Those long, shapely legs wrapped around him. It was a dream come true, the torment of his nightly yearnings turning to sweet bliss. Their bodies touched, then, without conscious effort on his part, merged.

"Oh," she whispered, closing her eyes tightly.

He couldn't hold out any longer as he felt her seductive movements against him, driving him onward. He closed his eyes and kissed her, feeling the full impact of her with all his senses. It was the best thing he'd ever experienced. He wanted it to be the same for her.

Jessica nipped at Clyde's shoulder, then kissed each spot, then nipped some more as restless hunger seized her. She met his every thrust and felt a thousand sparkles of delight run over her senses at his gentle caresses.

She heard the sounds of their breathing as they moved in concert, each second building on the next until she was panting with wild exhilaration. Then, like a shaken champagne bottle, she was filled to the bursting point.

"Yes," she cried softly when she finally came. "Oh, yes. Yes!"

She heard his groan of completion, then there was silence, except for the pounding of their hearts against each other, for long, delicious minutes.

The afternoon breeze gave the tree leaves a playful shake. Jessica felt the dappled sunlight like warm fingers on her face and half her body. Clyde had shifted to the side and rested with one leg and arm thrown protectively across her. She felt totally safe for the first time in months.

Sleep, deep and restful, crept over her. When she awoke, she was alone.

Sitting up, she spotted Clyde in the water, doing a lazy crawl along the length of the lake. That seemed like a good idea. She rose and waded in. At waist deep, she began swimming across the lake.

On the return, he joined her, swimming beside her and matching her stroke for stroke. After five laps, she stopped and treaded water in the middle, where the lake was over her head. He swam close, then she felt his powerful legs lock around hers, and they both went under.

Before she could splutter indignantly at the dunking, his mouth found hers. The kiss was deeply satisfying.

Against her hip, she felt the return of his passion and turned instinctively toward it, surprised that she could want him again so soon.

With long swipes of his arms, he swam on his back, taking them to shallow water. There, in the lapping wavelets against the sand, they made love again, slower, more perfect than the first time.

A long time later, he rose and held out his hand to her. "It's time to go in," he said.

She saw the sun had set. The sky was getting dark and the air cool. She heard the drone of a mosquito. "Yes."

He gave her the towel to dry off. He dressed quickly, but she was finished first. When she glanced at him, she saw the brooding darkness had returned to his eyes. The magic moment was truly over.

He collected the picnic basket, the tarp and the towel and stored them in the pickup. "Ready?"

She nodded and climbed in the passenger side without help. He drove silently back to the house. There he paused before getting out after he turned off the engine, his eyes even darker in the twilight.

"I knew you were a temptation when I spotted you at the airport that first day. I just didn't realize how irresistible you would be. I should have been on guard."

She felt his anger as a physical force. It wasn't directed at her so much as at himself. For being weak and giving in to their desire? The insult and hurt of it lodged deep within her psyche.

Lifting her chin, she regarded him without emotion.

"This afternoon was a very enjoyable interlude, but I don't expect it to change either of our lives."

With that, she hopped out of the truck and went to the house. Upstairs, under the hot shower, she vowed to put the moment of insane passion behind her and to never let herself be vulnerable to any man again.

After all, it wasn't as if she'd let herself fall for him or anything serious like that.

Five

On Thursday, Jessica lazed on the patio in the sun, its warmth soothing the tangled mix of emotions that had haunted her since Monday and the mindless interlude down by the lake.

For the thousandth time, she wondered how she could have been so lost to common sense and her usual caution around men. She mentally winced each time she thought of those ecstatic moments in Clyde's arms. Losing her head was so unlike her.

She was pretty sure it was the same for him. Okay, so they'd both succumbed to an irresistible attraction. Doing a lengthy postmortem didn't clear up any of the hazy thoughts that whirled through her brain.

So. She wouldn't think about it again.

Ha, easier said than done. She flopped over onto her tummy. Her hand hit something soft and furry.

"Hey, Smoky," she murmured, opening her eyes.

The dog wagged his tail and pranced around the patio, inviting her for a romp.

"Okay, let me get some shoes on," she told him.

Going into the house, she quickly changed from her swimsuit to cropped pants and a T-shirt and donned a pair of sneakers. Soon she and Smoky wandered about the grounds. She stopped to pull a few weeds she spotted in the shrub and perennial beds in front of the house and along the walkways.

Lavender, sage, basil, thyme and several other herbs she didn't recognize were planted near the kitchen. She wondered who took care of them. She'd seen no one working in the yard.

"Pixies?" she asked the dog, who wagged his tail and looked wise.

Following the dog, she wandered past the stable, which was empty, and stopped in front of a rustic shed. Hearing a cat's meow, she went inside, shutting the dog out.

"Oh," she murmured. Stooping, she peered under an old table at a mother cat and three kittens, the little ones looking like fuzzy balls of black, yellow and white.

She resisted picking them up, although they were so darling. Instead she stood. Glancing around the shed, she notices piles of furniture stacked to the ceiling.

The carved table sheltering the cat family caught her eye. It was old and scarred, yet the detail of the work was exquisite. With a little work, it would look lovely in the foyer of the main house.

Mmm, maybe she should point that out to Clyde. He might not be aware of the piece out here going to waste.

She and Smoky continued their roaming. They went down to the creek and found a stepping stone path across it. Going up the hill beyond the stream, a long barn, surrounded by green fields and a high fence, came into view.

Inside the fence were hundreds of chickens, pecking and cackling as they searched for food.

Spotting a man using a hose to rinse off his boots, she went down the slope and called out a hello. Beside him was a wheelbarrow filled with eggs.

"Hello," he answered her friendly greeting. "You must be Clyde's guest."

The man was in his early forties, she estimated, perhaps Latino and Native American mix. He had a thin, leathery face, an almost gaunt build and a brilliant smile.

"Uh, in a manner of speaking," she said, returning the smile as a shiver went down her spine. "I'm Jessica."

"Clinton Perez," the man said with a nod of his head.

From talking to Clyde's mother, she'd learned Clinton was a cousin to Ruben Perez, the gardener on Ryan Fortune's ranch. Rosita, Ruben's wife and the Double Crown housekeeper, was the woman who had seen the red ring around the moon before the body of Christopher Jamison had been discovered.

"You must be the foreman in charge of the egg operation," she said.

"Right. My wife Cimma and I, along with our two kids, collect and deliver free-range eggs to several restaurants in San Antonio."

"I know a free-range chicken is allowed to wander around and eat insects or whatever on its own. What do free-range eggs do?"

He turned off the water and looped the hose over the faucet. His deep chuckle was pleasant. "They come from free-range hens. If you've eaten any eggs since you've been here, you might have noticed the deep gold of the yolks. That's because the chickens are outside in the sunlight, absorbing Vitamin D. Through insects, they get other protein besides that from the chicken feed."

Jessica fell into step beside him when he wheeled the barrow of eggs to a concrete block building. Inside, it was cool, the light from high windows dim.

"Now I wash the eggs," he told her as if continuing a lecture. He placed the eggs in colanders, each holding three or four dozen, and ran them under a spray of water.

Next he flicked a switch and light appeared under a sheet of white plastic that formed the top of an otherwise metal table. He checked each egg against this backdrop.

"My grandmother raised chickens and sold eggs," she told the foreman. "She used a lightbulb to check for double yolks or fertilized eggs."

"We don't have roosters, so there'd better not be any fertilized eggs," he told her with a grain of wry humor. "But I do check for double yolks. For some reason, people don't like eggs to be different from each other."

"May I help? I liked doing that for Gran."

"Sure. My wife usually does this part, but she's not feeling well today."

Jessica took Clinton's place at the light table while he resumed washing the eggs. "I hope it isn't anything serious," she said politely.

"She'll be fine." He hesitated. "She miscarried two days ago. It's probably just as well. At our age, we hadn't planned on having more, but once we'd accepted the idea, the whole family was looking forward to a new little one. Now we're disappointed."

"Oh, I'm sorry," she murmured, sympathetic at the loss of the baby.

At once her mind reverted to Monday. She recalled she'd been spotted by this man while frolicking in the creek with the dog. Her face heated as she wondered if the foreman had also seen her and Clyde in the lake.

"Are your children in school?" she asked to divert the conversation to safer channels.

"Yes. They're teenagers. Our son is a senior and our daughter is a sophomore. They're in the FFA program. Both are studying farm management."

Jessica recalled that FFA stood for Future Farmers of America. Her grandmother had told her that once only boys could belong to the organization, which Jessica had thought very odd. She knew two classmates, both female, who'd taken over their family ranches when their parents had retired.

For the next hour she worked alongside Clinton. When they finished all the eggs, he thanked her and complimented her on her good work. "Now for the next load," he said and, lifting the handles on the wheelbarrow, headed outside.

"Do you have a lot of eggs?" she asked.

"Around two thousand on a good day."

Her mouth dropped in amazement.

Clinton laughed. "Hey, Clyde," he called. "Jessica is a pretty good worker. Maybe we ought to hire her before someone else snatches her up."

Her heart started going lickety-split upon seeing her host coming toward them. Other than the briefest of meetings in the hall or kitchen, she hadn't laid eyes on her host since…well, since the ill-advised episode at the lake.

He smiled, but there was a scowl in his eyes as he checked her over. "I don't think she needs our money. She has plenty of her own." He spoke to her. "I wondered where you'd gotten to. Maybe we need to arrange for a message center."

"My family always left notes on the refrigerator when I was growing up," she told him. "I suppose we could do that. Smoky and I were out for a walk. I didn't think about where we were going or how long we would be gone. I assumed we would be safe enough anywhere on the ranch."

She caught the slightly perplexed glance as Clinton's dark eyes flicked from one to the other.

"Yeah, you should be," Clyde agreed. The tension eased from his shoulders. "Ready to head for the house?"

Nodding, she bid the other man goodbye and fell into step with Clyde. Noticing a cat lying on the porch of the foreman's house, she told him about the kittens in the shed.

"There's also a table in there," she said, unable to hide her enthusiasm as she described the intricate carving. "It would look wonderful in the foyer when you first come in the front door."

"Huh," he said.

"I've redone some pieces that Mom and I sold at the hardware store. I could refinish the table. If you would like," she added at his silence.

"It's messy," he finally said. "It'll probably need stripping and some repairs before it can be stained and varnished again."

"I enjoy doing things like that," she said, immediately planning the project.

He studied her for a long minute before opening the kitchen door and letting her precede him into the house. "Fine. I suppose you need something to fill your time."

She wondered if that was what he thought of their moments at the lake—something to fill the time of an otherwise boring afternoon. She swallowed hard but the knot in her throat refused to dissolve.

"Yes," she said when she could speak, "it would be something interesting to fill the time."

Although she could think of other things....

Morning dawned gloriously bright. Jessica, full of plans, bustled out of bed and down the stairs in record time. Clyde was in the kitchen, sitting at the island and drinking coffee.

"Well, hello," she said after a flash of surprise. Noting his distant manner and dark expression, some perverse nature, hidden deep within, surfaced. She smiled brilliantly at him, then fluttered her eyelashes.

His dark eyebrows shot up, then dropped. He narrowed his eyes as he studied her old cut-off jeans and a faded T-shirt from some forgotten trip to a far corner of the globe.

"Are those your work clothes?" he asked.

"Yes. I want to start on the table while it's cool. Is there a room in the barn or stable where I can work?" She removed one egg from the refrigerator, paused, then held up another one with a question in her eyes.

He shook his head to the offer of breakfast. "I thought the arbor next to the guesthouse would be a good place. It's shady all day and usually pleasant. There's an electrical outlet and a faucet on that wall."

"That sounds perfect."

"I've put a tarp down on the tiles."

"Could you help me with the table before you leave?"

"It's already there. I bought a bottle of stripper, a scraper and rubber gloves in town yesterday afternoon. Your sister recommended the items."

"Oh." Jessica was seized with a bout of homesickness. "How is she? Did you see the girls? Were they all okay?"

"Leslie seemed fine. Also your brother-in-law. Your nieces weren't there."

"They have a lot of after-school functions." Jessica sighed. "It's odd to be so close and yet unable to see them. I feel as if I'm in some kind of prison."

He flicked her a glance from those dark, see-everything Heathcliff eyes.

"A very elegant prison," she quickly added.

"But still, a prison," he murmured, his eyes locking with hers.

"Not really." She scrambled the egg while the bread toasted, then took her seat at the counter. "I know I can leave at any time, but I…I don't want to. It's so nice not having to dread the ring of the phone."

"Don't you have a cell phone?"

"Usually, but I turned it in before I left New York. Roy had that number, too. Sondra is getting me another one in her name."

"Being a celebrity is tough."

His tone was noncommittal, so she couldn't tell if he was being sardonic or sympathetic. She shrugged.

"But you learn to handle it, I suppose, when guys come on to you all the time," he continued.

"Yes," she said coolly. "However, that's usually the least of your problems. Unless you run into a nutcase like Roy."

"What's the biggest problem?"

Seeing that he appeared serious, she answered in the same vein. "Fads, for one thing. I've seen people who were tops at seventeen and finished at twenty because they no longer epitomized the current fashion."

"That didn't happen to you."

"I've been lucky," she admitted. And she worked hard, but she didn't say that. "Time is the biggest problem. I'm thirty-three, nearly ancient in the high-fashion world."

"So what do you want to do with the rest of your life?"

"The usual. Settle down. Marry. Have a family."

He nearly choked on his coffee. She grinned when he cast her a doubtful look.

"Hey, you can take the girl out of the country…"

"But you can't take the country out of the girl," he finished when she stopped.

She nodded. "Being here has made me realize how much I miss my family. I'm booked for some major photo sessions for two more years, then, unless it's something really special, I plan to retire and raise petunias."

He gave a snort, which she assumed was amusement.

"Well," she said, "I'm ready to start on the table."

After straightening the kitchen, she headed outside. Smoky, her most constant companion, rushed over to greet her. She patted his head and promised him a walk later in the day. "For now I want to get to work. This table is a work of art. Do you know who carved it?" she asked Clyde.

"The rancher who owned this place. He used the shed as a workshop when his son took over the ranching chores. When he died, I think the furniture was stored and his son's wife bought new stuff. The wife sold to us, lock, stock and barrel, after her husband died."

"Would it be okay if I looked through the shed? I saw a rocking chair that has possibilities."

"Be my guest."

After brushing on a thick layer of furniture stripper, she spread an old newspaper over it to keep it from drying too fast. Clyde observed, which made her nervous. He finally said he'd see her later and left to deal with the increasing herd of cattle around the main house.

Although she'd never lived on a ranch, she knew the work involved. Clyde had tagged the heifers he wanted to keep and used a marker to write the numbers in their ears in case they lost the tags, which looked like flashy bright orange earrings each time the heifers flicked their ears.

A rancher had to be on the lookout for signs of illness, too—flies, parasites, worms, pink eye, tangles with thorns and barbed wire. Then there were mad cow disease and interesting things like that.

She returned to the shed after he left in the pickup. It took several minutes to move items so she could get the rocker free. During the process, she discovered a magazine holder and a neat chest with eight drawers, both carved similarly to the table. It was like striking gold.

"Wow," she murmured.

Carrying her treasures to the stripping area, she worked happily through the day, removing layers of grime and old varnish, then stopped to take Smoky for the promised walk late in the afternoon.

On an impulse, she picked a bouquet of flowers and carried them back to the house. She found the vase Clyde's mom had used and placed the arrangement on the dining table.

After a hot soak to smooth the kinks out of her back—from now on, she would stop and stretch for five minutes out of every hour while she worked—she dressed in black slacks and a black peasant blouse embroidered with golden squash blossoms around the neck and sleeves.

On an impulse, she decided to prepare dinner, just to show Clyde what a country girl could do, if she chose.

Clyde stopped at the gate and sniffed like an animal scenting trouble on the air. From the house came the delectable odors of food. Hot food.

His mouth actually watered. Other than the times his parents visited, a hot meal, ready when he came in, wasn't the norm in his household. He rushed to the house with the eagerness of a schoolboy looking for a treat.

"Hi, you're just in time," Jessica greeted him when he came in the back door. "Dinner in fifteen minutes. Will that give you enough time to shower?"

"Uh, yes."

Because his heart was dancing around like a whirling dervish, he frowned at her. Her smile faded, but she gave him one of her level, don't-mess-with-me stares.

He wondered how she could remain so cool while his blood heated to boiling. Bounding up the steps two at a time, he berated himself for the eagerness, for the desire raging through him and for a longing he couldn't describe.

While he showered, he reminded himself of all the reasons he was *not* going to get involved with her.

His mind heard, but his libido didn't listen.

Back downstairs, he found the formal table set with colorful dishes his mother had brought back from a trip to one of the flea markets in San Antonio. A vase, painted with a macaw and jungle flowers, was filled with flowers and held pride of place in the center of the table.

"Very nice," he managed to mutter past the strange obstacle in his throat.

Jessica, he noted, was playing the role of domesticated lady of the house to perfection.

"Everything is ready," she announced, bringing a basket of hot rolls to the table.

He suppressed the urgent and nearly overpowering need to kiss her on the back of the neck—right at that delicate spot below her ear. Instead he gallantly held her chair, then took the other seat at the end of the table.

"I prepared extra in case Miles came in, but I haven't seen any sign of him," she said. "This being Friday night, I thought he might, uh, go to town."

"We don't date during roundup," Clyde informed her.

"Or any other time?"

Those bright blue eyes dissected him while she waited for his answer. He forced a smile. "Miles has a string of females in three counties waiting for his call. I—"

He paused, not sure how much he wanted to disclose.

Sure, he dated some. The new librarian at the local high school. She'd married the football coach last Christmas after explaining that seeing *him* was a dead-end affair.

A pretty waitress at Emma's Café, although he was leery of waitresses after his youthful encounter and heartbreak. However, she'd run off with a cowboy last spring. It must have been love at first sight.

"I don't go out much," he concluded. "Too busy."

Too wise, some part of him added. Yeah. He'd learned the hard way about trusting his heart to a woman, especially one like Jessica. She looked like an exotic flower, just waiting to be plucked. And caressed. And kissed until they were both breathless.

"Aren't you hungry?" she asked.

Setting his jaw, he forked a tender piece of chicken onto his plate, added a baked potato and a mixture of vegetables. He recognized fresh herbs from the garden whipped into a cream sauce that was part of the veggie dish. It was different.

"Delicious," he told her—and meant it—after the meal. "Maybe you can get a job as a chef in a fancy restaurant after you retire from modeling."

"Well," she said with surprising modesty, "I've been studying finance with an eye toward being a certified advisor. I realized I had to learn how to handle money when I started earning big bucks, so I started taking courses every chance I got."

"You should talk to my father, then. He might need someone—" He stopped when she shook her head.

"I want to move back to Texas," she told him.

"You could open a modeling school," he suggested and wondered why he insisted on seeing her as a celebrity.

"Or a furniture refinishing business. That was what I was thinking of doing before Violet talked me into applying for a scholarship to the university where she was going."

"You're kidding," he said in open disbelief.

"Nope. Mom and I really enjoy taking something old and making it new and usable again. She and Dad have an antique shop in Austin. Maybe I should go into business with them."

He shook his head. "I can't picture that."

In fact, he couldn't find a middle ground between the lanky, shy girl she'd once been and the poised model who'd traveled all over the world and had a man so obsessed, she'd had to hide out to escape him.

"Did you see how lovely the table turned out?" she asked. "I think a natural stain to bring out the golden tones of the oak would be nice. Do you prefer oil- or water-based sealer? Mom says oil is the best, but water is so much easier to clean up."

"The water-based stuff seems to work fine."

"I thought so, too."

Finished, they took their dishes to the kitchen and, together, put them away. He'd never done domestic things with a woman before. It felt...pleasant.

They returned to the table with fresh pear tarts she'd found in the freezer and baked. When he finished that, he felt full and satisfied. Almost.

He forced his mind away from images of how they might sate the sexual hunger that hummed through them. He wondered if she was aware of it as much as he was.

"Look, Smoky is chasing a bee," she said, peering out the window. "I hope for his sake he doesn't catch it." She laughed as the dog leaped into the air after the bumblebee.

Clyde liked the way her eyes crinkled at the corners and the way two little lines bracketed her mouth. He liked the soft, buttery sound of her laughter, the bright intelligence of her eyes that reminded him of an alert robin hopping about the lawn on a perfect spring day, the way her scent drifted to him each time she moved.

He knew just where she wore perfume. At the vulnerable spot below her ear, at her throat and between her breasts. In the crook of her arms, behind her knees. On the delicate Venus mound that led to the sweetest treasure he'd ever known.

Hunger surged to a roaring inferno. He wanted to kiss her, to sweep her into his arms like a hero in a melodrama and carry her up the stairs to his room. He wanted to keep her with him all night and make love whenever they woke, no matter the hour.

Instead, he cleared his throat and stood. "Excuse me," he said, "I have things to do. The dinner was nice, but it isn't necessary for you to cook, since we never know when we'll get in."

"Well," she said reasonably, "as long as I'm cooking for me, I can fix more. That way you or Miles can heat it in the microwave when you do get a chance to eat."

Her smile reminded him of things that would never be, like those youthful dreams of having a great love and a good marriage the way his parents did. "We don't have time to play admirers of your many skills," he said in a snarl.

The pleasure fled from her eyes and was replaced with something like shock. It quickly disappeared, too. Behind a shield of perfect composure, she nodded. "I didn't mean you were obligated to…to…"

A frown nicked a tiny line between her eyebrows as her voice trailed off.

"I'll take care of the dessert plates," she ended.

Nodding, he headed for his room and the computer, where a stack of data waited to be entered on each breeding cow in the herd. That should keep him busy for hours…and away from potential trouble.

Six

Jessica sliced carrots over the bowl of lettuce, added a small cucumber and green onions, then mixed the salad with a vinaigrette dressing. The telephone rang just as she plopped down on the stool at the counter.

Since it wasn't her house, she let the answering machine pick up the call.

"Jessica? Are you there?" she heard Violet ask.

She rushed to the phone. "Hello? Violet? Where in the world are you?"

Her friend laughed. "I'm not sure. Somewhere in the ocean on a cruise ship that looks like a wedding cake."

"When your mother told me you actually did take a cruise, I was flabbergasted. I didn't believe it when you said you were thinking seriously of going off on one."

Violet's sigh came through loud and clear. "I wanted to get away, all by myself, and just think."

"I know what you mean," Jessica said. "It's been won-derful here. Quiet. Peaceful."

She felt a bit uncomfortable at the lie. Well, it had been peaceful around the house the past week. The turmoil had all been inside her.

Clyde had swapped jobs with Miles and stayed in the back country rounding up strays while Miles sorted cattle and loaded the sales stock onto the huge trucks that came regularly every other afternoon.

"Are my brothers treating you right?" Violet demanded.

"Of course. Miles and I have an ongoing game of gin rummy nearly every night. Since I'm ahead, he won't quit."

"He likes to win," Violet said, laughter in her voice. "Uh, where's Clyde?"

"Out in the back forty."

"Mmm, usually he does the wheeling and dealing with the buyers, also the computer stuff. Miles likes to be out in the wide-open spaces."

Jessica pressed her lips firmly together, suppressing a need to tell her best friend all that had happened between her and the oldest brother of the triplets.

"So what are you doing to keep yourself busy?"

Jessica enthusiastically launched into her great discov-ery in the shed and the results of her efforts on the furni-ture. "It really came out nice. Miles and I put the table and chest in the foyer, and the rocking chair and magazine rack in the empty room."

"Mmm, you're sounding very domesticated," Violet said.

"I'd forgotten what fun Mom and I used to have with our recycled 'treasures,' as we called them. I think there's enough furniture in the shed to make an office for the ranch in the spare room, if your brothers would like that. Miles has given his approval, but I haven't had a chance to ask Clyde yet."

"Sounds nice. Clyde could then move the computer and files out of his bedroom."

"Uh, yes." Jessica had gone upstairs to search the shelves for a new book to read one night last weekend and spotted Clyde working in his room through the open door.

His bedroom was nearly a replica of hers, except the bed appeared to be larger. Images of sharing it with him had driven her down the steps and outside until her blood had cooled and the lightness had disappeared from her brain.

"I'm about to forget why I called. Have you had any calls from our favorite stalker?" Violet asked.

"None. I've hardly been off the ranch since I arrived." She realized it was Friday and it had been exactly two weeks ago that she'd arrived in a driving rainstorm. She'd been at the ranch only three days when she and Clyde had...

She hesitated over a descriptive term and mentally changed "made love" to "had that episode at the lake."

"I can't tell you what a relief it's been not to have to deal with Roy and his obsession," she concluded.

"Have you seen your parents?"

"No. I'm following our plan. I do miss them, though," Jessica admitted. "I'm thinking of moving back here."

"You're not!" Violet said in surprise.

"Yes, I am. It's time we were settling down, old friend," she said, reminding Violet that they weren't getting any younger. They'd discussed this very thing when they'd turned thirty and decided they should start seriously looking for their dream mates.

"Who with?" Violet asked glumly.

"I don't know. I do know I want my kids to know their grandparents on both sides." She laughed softly. "So I'll have to marry a Texas man and settle here."

"Hey, we were going to raise our kids together."

"Well, you'll have to find a Texas man, too. Hold on," she said to her friend, hearing something behind her.

Clyde stood on the threshold of the back door, glaring at her in his best Heathcliff imitation. She wondered how much of her conversation he'd heard.

"Your brother's here," she told Violet, ignoring his moody scowl. "You want to talk to him?"

"I suppose I'll have to," her friend said, pretending to be reluctant to do so.

Jessica handed over the phone.

"Hey, where are you?" Clyde asked. He rummaged around in a kitchen drawer until he found the item he was looking for, an air needle to blow up the Perez kid's basketball.

As his sister told him of her cruise and the ports she'd visited, he was intensely aware of Jessica at the counter. She ate from a large bowl of salad, her eyes on the food as if this was the only thing that occupied her thoughts.

Being anywhere near her drove him right up the wall!

That was why he'd forced Miles to change places with him. He'd needed to get away from the house this past week. Not that it had helped a whole lot. His every thought, waking or sleeping, was of the woman who now silently ate and totally ignored his presence.

"Are you keeping an eye on Jessica?" his sister asked.

"Yes."

"How?" she demanded. "Jessica said you were directing the roundup while Miles stayed at the house."

"Well, he's watching over her. I explained the problem to him."

"You promised you would do it."

Other than his mom when she was on one of her crusades, he'd never known anyone as stubborn as his kid sister. "She's fine, isn't she?" he demanded.

"So far." Her tone changed, becoming pensive. "I listened to the tapes of Roy's calls. It was spooky. He truly is obsessed."

"Yeah, well, everything is fine here. Are you having a good time?"

"I suppose." She sighed. "I'm rethinking my life."

A ripple of concern went through him. This wasn't like the sister he knew. "I thought medicine was your life."

"It is. It was. People die. That makes it hard."

"You can't blame yourself. You do the best you can. That's all anyone can do."

"I know." Her sigh was despondent. "This call is costing a fortune, so I'll hang up. Take care of Jessica. And yourself."

After he replaced the phone, he paused and checked his house guest over visually. There was a light tan on her face and arms from the hours she'd spent outside. She'd helped at the egg barn for three or four hours each afternoon of the past week, until the Perez kids got home from school.

Miles had also reported that each morning she'd devoted herself to refinishing the furniture and the pieces were now in place in the house. There were flowers in a vase on the windowsill over the sink, too.

The ranch house was becoming very homey. He scoffed silently. As if it made any difference to him. She'd be gone soon and his life would get back to normal.

"Miles has gone into San Antonio," he now said to their guest. "He'll probably spend the night."

She nodded as if she knew this.

"I have some work to do on the tractor. I'll be out at the hay barn for a couple of hours." He hesitated. "Will you be okay here alone?"

"Of course." She gave him one of her charming smiles.

His heart lurched around like a dizzy boxer who'd taken one punch too many. He nodded grimly and headed outside.

Jessica put her bowl and fork in the dishwasher, then leaned against the sink. Outside, Clyde called to someone. When the Perez boy came forward, the two males went to the barn where Clyde used a compressor to blow up a flat basketball.

The teenager bounced the ball a couple of times, smiled and headed for his place with a wave. Clyde bent over the big tractor that served many purposes on the ranch.

She watched him work on it for a long time, wishing she felt poised enough to go talk to him while he did. With Miles, she wouldn't have hesitated. They shared an easy relationship that had enlivened the evenings while they played cards and joked with each other.

Unfortunately there was no spark, only a pleasing friendship that worked for both of them. After thinking about this, she gave up trying to figure out why one person appealed to another, and went upstairs.

She'd showered earlier, after working in the egg barn all afternoon. She and Cimma Perez, who was on her feet again, had formed a good team at cleaning and checking the eggs while Clinton kept them in fresh supply.

After changing into a nightgown, she climbed into bed, opened the book she'd borrowed and read of the "true life" adventures of a cowboy who'd lived at the turn of the twentieth century.

At ten, she closed the book and turned out the light, fairly certain the adventures had been true only in the mind of the man who'd claimed to live them. Ah, well, everyone had dreams.

Clyde, she noted, hadn't come in the house yet. Before he'd changed places with Miles, he'd been up in the mornings before she rose and hadn't come in until she was in bed.

He probably made sure her light was out before he dared creep inside and up the stairs. Did he think she was wait-

ing to pounce on him or lure him to her room with her
deadly charms?

Ha! He could think again!

She closed her eyes and determinedly counted sheep
until she heard his quiet steps on the stairs. Then she fell
into a restful sleep.

Jessica was startled upon seeing Clyde still in the
kitchen when she went down Monday morning. "Hello,"
she said, tingly and uneasy at his presence.

"Good morning," he said and resumed reading the paper.

She ate her usual sparse meal, then settled at the counter
with a fresh cup of coffee and selected a section of the
paper to read. Thirty minutes passed in silence.

When he put the paper down, she did, too. She glanced
outside. Clouds were on the horizon, dark and heavy gray.
The weather channel had predicted a storm front would be
in today.

"Looks as if the storm is on its way," she said.

"Yeah."

"Aren't you heading out to the far pastures again?"

"No."

At his short answer, she nodded calmly.

"I'll have a few days off while the crew is doing some
fence repairs before starting on a new sector," he said.

Miles had explained they used a temporary crew to help
with the roundup each fall and the calf count each spring,
but normally the brothers and a couple of cowboys who
lived on the other side of the ranch did the rest of the work.

"What were you planning to do today?" Clyde asked.

She shrugged. "Read, I suppose, and hide from the
housekeeper this morning. I was going to work on some
furniture for the ranch office—"

"What ranch office?"

"The one Miles and I planned this past week." She grinned at her host's frown. "The room on the other side of the dining area was empty, so I put the rocking chair and magazine rack in there. Miles realized it would be a good place for the ranch records so he and Steven wouldn't have to invade your room each time they needed to check on something."

The black, nearly straight eyebrows rose slightly. "That's a good idea."

Jessica nearly fell off the stool when he smiled.

"You finished?" he asked.

She nodded.

"Then let's get cracking. Today will be a good day to work inside."

To her amazement, he led the way upstairs and into his room. The bed wasn't exactly made, but the plaid comforter had been fluffed over the covers. She could detect bumps under it as if the sheets had been smoothed carelessly.

Under the windows along the north wall was a desk and two file cabinets and another, taller cabinet, its doors open to reveal several pieces of equipment that went with the computer on the desk.

"Let's take the drawers out of the file cabinets and move them first, then I'll disconnect the electronic stuff."

He seemed enthusiastic about the task, so she pitched in and helped. Instead of letting her carry the drawers neatly filled with manila folders and hanging files, he brought in a dolly from the storage shed. Together they loaded it and gently eased the dolly down the steps and into the room now designated as the office. That was where the housekeeper, a woman she didn't know, found them.

After a quick introduction to the older woman, Clyde turned to Jessica. "Where do you want the file cabinets?"

"Here," she said, going to the back wall. "We'll put the

desk facing the windows, so you…or whoever is working," she added, "can see the barns and pastures."

He nodded.

It took a couple of hours to get everything down the steps and into the room, then a couple more for him to re-connect the computer parts and check everything out.

She removed a calendar and a dry erase board from the wall of his bedroom and put them on the inside of the doors of the computer cabinet. "There," she told him, "these will be handy, yet out of sight."

He glanced up from the monitor, where flashing num-bers indicated a file defragmentation check was taking place. "Good." His grin was one of satisfaction. "Thanks for your help. I've been meaning to do this for ages, but…"

At his shrug, she said, "You never found the time."

"None of us made the time," he corrected. He looked at his watch. "It's one o'clock. We haven't had lunch."

"I'll fix sandwiches," she volunteered, then recalled he didn't want her doing anything for him.

His perusal was thoughtful. "You haven't been away from the ranch since the funeral. There's a great barbecue place just south of San Antonio. It should be safe to go there. I don't think anyone will recognize you."

"They don't keep up with the latest fashions?" she asked as if deeply shocked.

"Not the ones in New York. Now, Texas style, that's a different story. You're dressed just right for that."

Like him, she wore jeans and a chambray shirt, the cuffs rolled up. However, she wore sandals rather than boots. Her toenails were painted a rosy pink like her fingernails, which she'd manicured the previous day.

She ran upstairs for her purse, said goodbye to the housekeeper, then joined him in the pickup. The wind was whipping up dust devils, but the rain hadn't yet arrived.

"Maybe the storm will miss us," she said, eyeing the clouds as their pickup sped west on the state road.

"Not a chance. We'll eat, then head back. I think we're in for a rainy night."

"Did Miles go back out on the range?" She thought of wind and flash floods, both dangerous things that could overturn an RV.

"He's in Austin, taking care of some paperwork with Steven. He'll be back tomorrow."

A chill settled on her neck. She and Clyde would have the house to themselves tonight. That made her nervous. Sort of, she added as a thrill rushed through her. Or maybe it made her excited.

"So you won't have long to miss him," he finished.

"He's nice. Fun, too. But I won't miss him," she said with complete honesty.

"Huh," he said, a note of disbelief in the word.

"When I moved out on my own in New York, I learned not to depend on anyone else for my entertainment. That's especially true when I go out of the country for a fashion show. Hotel rooms all look the same after a while."

"Violet said you go to Paris and Milan each year. Don't you have lots of social engagements then?"

She laughed. "Hardly. We work long hours. When we're not working, we get as much rest as we can so we're fresh for the next day. The month leading up to fashion week, plus that week, is the most hectic time in the life of a model. I sleep for another week when it's over."

"So you don't have time to date the cosmopolitan types who hang out at the shows?"

"No. Most of us don't want to, either."

They arrived at a restaurant and pulled into the pot-holed parking lot. It looked like a honky-tonk.

When Clyde took her arm before they went inside the

wooden doors that looked as if they belonged on a barn, she instinctively moved closer. His warmth seeped into her left side. He chose a booth with red seats and red plastic covers on the table. The window panes had been painted blue so no one could see in or out.

"Quaint," she murmured, then grinned at him. "It is nice to be out on the town, so to speak."

A cowboy, complete with jeans, boots and a ten-gallon hat, dropped coins into a jukebox. Country music filled the very dim interior. Jessica relaxed. No one would recognize her here, not unless they used a flashlight.

She smothered a laugh.

Clyde smiled at her as the gum-popping waitress brought over menus and tall glasses of water.

"Somep'm-ta-drink?" she asked, running the words into one.

"Iced tea," he said.

Jessica seconded the choice. After the young woman left, she sank back in the comfortable booth and sighed. "Ah, it's good to be home."

"You have missed it," he said, sounding surprised.

"Yes."

Their eyes met. A slow, moody love song wafted from the speaker mounted in the ceiling. The cowboy who'd selected the music led his girl onto the hardwood floor, and they did the Texas two-step with expertise.

"My father taught me and my sister the two-step when I was ten and she was six. I remember being amazed when he and my mother danced. They were really good."

"It's surprising what old people know, isn't it?" her companion teased.

The waitress returned. Jessica ordered the rib platter when Clyde did. It came with cornbread, fries, baked beans and roadhouse slaw, made with corn kernels and hot peppers. She wondered if she could eat half the meal when the large platters of food arrived. She ate everything.

"My lips are burning," she said. "And my throat and tongue. I'm not used to jalapeno peppers anymore."

"Lots of things are different in your world, I imagine," he said in a musing tone.

"New York used to be your world," she reminded him.

"I opted out. My dad was disappointed that Steven, Miles and I decided to make our home in the Wild West."

"Your mother wasn't surprised."

"She said we belonged here." He smiled, then took a drink of iced tea.

Outside the storm hit with a sudden downpour that drummed on the metal roof of the building like a band of marching men. The temperature inside the rustic restaurant seemed to drop several degrees.

Jessica recalled that she'd blown in on a storm on the second of the month. It was now the nineteenth. Just then another realization came to her—and she nearly dropped her glass.

"Ready?" Clyde asked, seeming to see the restlessness that had seized her.

She hid any sudden nervousness and replied, "Yes." When she was alone later, she'd deal with her new problem.

He paid the bill and had her wait at the door while he pulled the vehicle close. She leaped inside as quickly as possible and slammed the door behind her, but even that didn't keep her dry.

"It's really coming down," she said, shaking off the rain.

He handed her a neatly folded white handkerchief. She wiped the moisture from her face and gave it back, her fingers trembling just a tiny bit.

The trip to the ranch house was accomplished in near silence, other than a comment or two about the wind, which whipped across the road in gusts that shook the pickup. Clyde kept a firm grasp on the steering wheel.

Jessica was relieved that the rain let up just as they arrived at the ranch. The sky had turned charcoal-gray so that it seemed deep twilight as they raced for the house.

Clyde opened the door and let her go in first. As soon as they were safely inside, the rain hit again with bansheelike force while the wind howled around the eaves.

"This is the type of storm that breeds tornadoes," he murmured, standing by the window and studying the clouds.

"I remember. That was what killed my grandparents when I was twelve. My father had wanted them to move to town and live with us, but my granddad wouldn't hear of it. They had a storm cellar, but they didn't get to it in time. The storm came during the night."

"I'm sorry," he said in his quiet baritone. "One of my grandfathers had a heart attack while we were visiting. It was a shock. I was a teenager and I'd never thought about them dying."

She nodded in understanding. They stood there for a minute, then she excused herself and went to her room. There, she removed the PDA from her purse and checked the calendar. After a minute of staring at it, she hit the off button and put it away.

As a model, there were certain things she carefully kept track of. Her monthly cycle was one of them. She was three days late.

Staring out the window at the wind lashing the trees along the creek, she could only murmur, "Dear heavens."

She didn't know if that was a prayer or a plea.

Seven

That evening, Clyde sat in the newly furnished office, but his mind wasn't on business. Jessica was in the family room, the television tuned to a local station as she watched the six o'clock news. He found himself listening for the slightest sound from her.

Grimacing at his own foolishness, he glanced out the window at the dark sky. He could tell what the weather was going to be without checking with a meteorologist, he thought, his spirits as gloomy as the climate.

The storm lashed the house intermittently, as if pausing every few minutes to catch its breath. It was the type of weather front that settled in close to the coast and stayed there for two or three or four days. Good thing there was a break in the roundup chores.

Hearing footsteps, he swung his gaze toward the open door. Jessica appeared in the kitchen. She glanced in his direction, then seemed disconcerted to find him observing.

"Uh, I'm going to have a cup of tea," she said, hesitated, then added, "You want one?"

He knew he should say no, but he nodded.

Cursing, he had to concede he had the willpower of an ant scenting a honey jar when it came to resisting her. However, he would *not* be a mindless slave to the attraction between them, powerful as it was. A man controlled his passions.

"Ready," she called out.

At some point during the past hour, she'd changed into the blue gown and lacy blue robe. He wondered if the gown had matching lace on it. Yeah, they were probably a set…probably given to her by some rich guy…probably after seeing her model it in one of those underwear shows—

He broke the train of thought with a low groan, forced himself out of the chair and went into the kitchen.

Her hair was clipped behind her ears with two silver clasps and flowed down her back in a cascade of shimmering honey-colored silk. He balled his hands to keep from touching it.

"I didn't put anything in your tea," she said, pouring nonfat milk into her cup. "Do you use milk?"

"No, sugar and lemon."

She returned the milk to the fridge and went back to the evening news. He trailed after her, liking the way the lacy robe and silky gown floated around her slender feet, barely clearing the floor. She wore the soft ballet slippers she preferred in the house.

When she settled onto the sofa with her feet tucked under her, she appeared surprised to see him. He took the chair and propped his sock-clad feet on the ottoman.

In a fancy mirror his mother had found at a yard sale and placed on the wall above the TV set, he could see their reflections in the cozy room. If not for the tension that hummed through him, the scene would have looked perfectly sedate and peaceful.

The lights of a vehicle on the driveway flashed into the room and were gone.

Clyde set his cup on the side table and went to see who had arrived. Expecting Miles, he was surprised to see his other triplet.

"Yo, Steven," he greeted his sibling, opening the back door, then closing it against the wind and rain when Steven was inside. "Man, you picked a good night to be out. What brings you down this way?"

"Business in San Antonio," Steven answered, shaking water off his hat into the sink, then hanging both hat and jacket on hooks by the door. "I thought I'd drop by while I was close and go over the contract with the new produce company." He glanced toward the foyer. "Miles said your house guest is still in residence?"

"Yes. Violet's friend, Jessica Miller," Clyde said firmly, feeling it necessary to make the connection clear.

"I remember her from the funeral. Her dad ran the hardware store in Red Rock, didn't he?"

"Yeah." Clyde was aware of Steven's eyes on him as he led the way into the new office.

"Very nice," his brother remarked after checking over the room. "Miles said Jessica was the one who finally got you to move everything into here."

"She found some furniture in the shed."

He followed Steven's gaze to the rocking chair, the magazine rack, now filled with ranching periodicals, and the black painted table that had joined the other two pieces yesterday.

A floor lamp, which she'd had him rewire, cast a soft light into the room each time he flicked on the wall switch. Its yellowed shade had been stained with tea, giving it an interesting textured appearance. An old basket, found in the loft of the barn, held sprays of dried grass she'd picked beside the road.

"She calls it shabby Texas chic," he explained.

Steven gave him a long, slow once-over, then grinned like an idiot.

"What?" Clyde asked irritably.

"Nothing. Not a thing, bro." He removed a sheaf of papers from an envelope and laid them on the desk, the surface of which was clear for once.

Together, they went over the contract for all the eggs the ranch could supply to the distributor. "The cash flow will be good next year," Clyde murmured, checking the figures against the old contract.

"Yeah, and here's the best part. The chefs are clamoring for free-range chickens to make stock for soups, so this will consolidate the market."

After an hour of planning and estimating next year's income and outgo, Clyde added his signature to the contract, then asked how Steven's new enterprises were going.

"Fine." His brother strode toward the door. "I'll say hello to Jessica. Amy gave me a message for her."

Annoyed without knowing why, Clyde followed Steven into the family room. Jessica hit the mute button on the TV and gave his brother her most charming smile. "It's good to see you again."

"How's it going?" Steven asked, settling on the sofa. "Are you getting plenty of rest and relaxation here?"

"Yes," she said. "This is a wonderful place. You should think about opening a bed and breakfast for harried families to visit."

"We have all we can handle at present," Steven told her. "I think you met my fiancée, Amy, didn't you?"

"Yes, at the funeral."

"Our house is finished and we'll be moving in as soon

as the furniture's delivered. We're planning a quiet wedding with just family because one of Amy's clients—"

"He's the governor," Clyde interrupted. "Amy helps plan his events."

"Yes, I remember," Jessica said. "Congratulations on your coming marriage," she said to Steven.

"Thanks. Anyway, we don't want a lot of publicity about the wedding, but Amy told me to tell you she would love it if you would come. Violet has promised she'll be back from her cruise in time."

"Well, uh, that's very nice of you," Jessica began, her eyes cutting to Clyde in uncertainty, "but I don't think I'll be here. I plan on leaving at the end of the month."

"Perfect," Steven said. "The wedding is scheduled for Friday, the last day of the month. We needed to fit it in with the governor's schedule, which isn't easy to do."

"I'll see that she gets there," Clyde said to his brother. He ignored her severe frown. "With Governor Meyers present, no one will notice one more beautiful woman," he assured her quietly.

She rolled her eyes.

Steven turned to him. "We're not having a fancy reception after the wedding. Just something small at our ranch. We're already involved with a really big event at our place to honor Ryan."

Clyde nodded. "You've mentioned that."

"That's how Amy and I met," Steven explained to Jessica. "If we have the big shindig, the governor will be giving Ryan an award for his charitable deeds, so Amy has to be in on the planning."

"If?" Clyde asked, picking up on the questioning note in his brother's statement.

Steven stretched his legs out and crossed them at the ankles, a troubled expression on his face. "Well, there's the question of who murdered Christopher Jamison and who had the most to lose or gain by it."

"And that's Ryan Fortune, who might not have wanted known the truth of his father's illegitimate birth and subsequent adoption by the Fortune family."

"Assuming Christopher threatened to expose the news," Steven added in disgust. "As if that would bother Ryan."

Clyde nodded. "I agree. Ryan would have more to lose by murdering someone than he would have to gain by suppressing the facts. Kingston is dead. His past doesn't affect Ryan's life or family in any way that I can see."

"It's really sad for someone in his prime to be killed," Jessica said in a musing tone. "From all accounts, Christopher was a really nice person."

"Probably ran into some nut at the lake." Clyde scowled at the thought.

"But why was he at the lake?" Steven questioned. "Or was he killed someplace else and brought to the lake close to the Double Crown Ranch so Ryan would be implicated?"

"With any luck the police will get to the bottom of it soon," Jessica said.

They were silent for a moment.

"So is the party on hold?" Clyde continued after considering the strange case and coming to no conclusions.

"Not exactly." Steven gave a humorless snort. "It would be rather awkward, though, if the guest of honor is arrested for murder during the proceedings."

Clyde paced the floor. "The cops wouldn't do that, not with the governor in attendance."

"One can only hope," his brother commented.

Steven rubbed a hand over his face and stood, telling them he still had the drive back to Austin and would keep in contact on the final time for the ceremony. Clyde realized Steven was tired and worried. Their lives had surely taken some unexpected turns of late, he thought.

After he saw Steven out, he returned to the family room. Picking up the cup, he took a sip of the cool tea and made a face.

"Heat it up in the microwave," Jessica suggested. "That's what I did."

He did so, then rummaged in the cabinet until he found a package of cookies. He brought the box into the family room. The television was off. Jessica was staring out the window at the rain-washed night, her eyes dark and pensive.

"Did talk of the murder bother you?" he asked.

"Some."

"Are you still worried about the stalker?"

She shook her head. "I think Violet was right—once I was out of sight, I was out of Roy's mind. He has nothing to gain by stalking me and everything to lose, such as the career he's so proud of. He's ambitious. I'm sure he has visions of being governor of New York one day."

Clyde grimaced. Politics weren't his thing.

"I'm sorry I've imposed on your hospitality," she continued. "I think I'll go visit my parents in Austin."

"No."

Her eyes flicked to him in surprise.

He realized he needed to come up with some explanation for his quick reaction, other than a gut feeling that she shouldn't leave, that it would be a mistake for reasons he couldn't quite articulate.

"We should stick with the plan," he told her. "Violet said you had another month of vacation. After the wedding, which will be in Austin, you can go home with your folks and visit with them. That will give the politician plenty of time to get over his obsession."

Her eyes brightened. "So you do believe me about that?"

"Oh, yes," he said wryly. He could certainly identify with the poor slob who'd fallen for her like the proverbial ton of bricks.

The next morning, Jessica checked her PDA again. Nope, no mistake. Like the thump of a bass drum in her head, she felt the hard pound of her blood, a slow dirge that signaled the worry that had grabbed her yesterday when she'd realized how late in the month it was.

A child!

She closed her eyes and slumped into the bedroom chair as if all her stuffing had fallen out in an instant.

What if there was a baby? And what if the stalker found her? Would it make him furious that she was expecting another man's offspring? If the baby was already born, would he hurt it as well as her?

Perhaps she was overreacting again. She'd watched too many of those true-crime reenactments on television. Maybe not all stalkers killed the object of their obsession.

She replaced the PDA in her purse, then went downstairs. The phone rang before she reached the back door, and she waited for the machine to answer.

After the recorded message, in Steven's voice, inviting the caller to leave his name and phone number, there was total silence on the line.

The hair rose on the back of her neck. She pulled in a deep breath with an effort. Oh, no, not again!

But then she heard the click of the disconnect and the answering machine turned itself off. The hush in the kitchen beat at her ears like a tom-tom. She checked the caller ID feature, but no number was recorded.

A wrong number. That's all. It was a wrong number.

She repeated this as she went outside. The humidity clamped down on her skin like a damp wool blanket, adding physical discomfort to the uneasy mixture of emotion inside her. She would not let a simple wrong number upset her.

Skirting the pool, she crossed the patio and headed toward the creek. A brisk walk would take care of the tension caused by an overactive imagination.

The grass was dry, she found, but the ground was spongy with moisture. The sky was still overcast and threatening more rain. For the moment, the wind had died down.

Hearing Smoky in the front yard, she ambled around the house and found Clyde squatting beside a flower bed. The dog retrieved the stick that had been thrown and brought it to her instead of Clyde, laying it at her feet.

She threw it and smiled as Smoky darted away then got distracted by a bumblebee and tried to snag it in midair by leaping as high as he could.

Glancing at her host, who was intent on pulling weeds, she wondered why she and Smoky were attracted to the very things that could hurt them—

She broke the thought. No one could hurt her, not if she kept her distance, and she'd gotten proficient at that.

"Good morning," she said with determined cheer.

He stood and tossed the uprooted grass into a plastic trash bag. "Good morning."

Tingles rushed along her nerves as his dark gaze slid over her. She wondered what a child of theirs would look like. Tall? Yes. Brown-eyed? Probably, since the darker color was dominant. Outgoing like its uncle Miles or quiet and introspective like its father? Boy or girl?

So many questions.

"What is it?" he asked, his eyes narrowing. "Is something wrong?"

She shook her head, realizing she'd been staring. If they were in love, the news of a child would be received with joy and excited plans for the future. On some instinctive level, she knew he wanted children, that he would be a kind, loving father and a wonderful husband.

"I, uh, was restless and thought I'd better get outside while the storm is in a lull." She glanced at the bag half-filled with pruned shrub branches and weeds. "I wondered who did the yard work. I assumed you had a landscape service."

His smile did things to her heart. "You're looking at it. Mom says working in the garden is good for the soul. I find it relaxing. Most of the time."

She wondered if the latter phrase was meant to exclude her presence. The tension grew to an almost audible hum in the air. During the awkward moment, she saw his hand clench, then relax, as if he forced himself not to react to it.

"Well, I'll let you get back to work," she said and hurried toward the line of trees marking the creek.

The sound of the stream was loud as she approached. She found the water murky and fast moving. At the dam, it rushed over the stones on top of the earthen structure. She decided to stay on this side of the creek and close to the house as the wind picked up again.

As she walked toward the homestead, she felt the first drops of rain hit her face and arms. Smoky joined her as she raced up the side lawn. Reminded of her youth and the happy days she'd spent at her grandparents' small ranch, she laughed as she and the dog tried to beat the storm.

The door opened just as she reached for the knob. The wind, as cold as a sudden frost, pushed her inside, and Clyde forced the portal closed while Smoky headed for shelter in the stable where he slept each night.

The onslaught of the storm was accompanied by a brief burst of hail that beat on the windows like mischievous demons trying to get inside.

"A foretaste of winter," she said, still smiling as she
dried off with a paper towel.

"Yeah."

"Did you finish your weeding?" she asked.

"No. Only half the front yard is done."

She wondered if she should have volunteered to help,
then decided that wasn't a good idea. She had to keep her
distance, she told herself firmly, although considering the
circumstances, it might be a little late for that.

Thunder boomed directly overhead, sounding like a
summons from hell. Every muscle in her body jerked. The
lights flickered, then went out. The gloom of the storm entered the room. Jessica wrapped her arms across her chest
as chill bumps danced along her skin.

"We can have a fire," he said.

He filled a coffee cup, then went into the family room.
She did the same and followed. The fireplace had a gas
starter, so in a matter of minutes cheery flames leaped over
the wood. He added several more logs from a supply located behind a handy door.

"Nice," she said from the corner of the sofa where she
usually sat.

He settled in his usual chair with a nod. When the phone
rang, he answered the extension on the table beside the
leather recliner. "Flying Aces," he said.

When he hung up without saying more, she asked,
"Wrong number?"

He shrugged. "I suppose. They hung up."

Him again? Jessica wondered. How had he found her?

Staring into the fire, she felt something akin to hopeless-
ness wash over her. The telephone calls and the possibility of an unplanned pregnancy weighed on her soul…and
her conscience.

If she hadn't fled to the wilds of Texas like a coward,

none of this would be happening. "I'm sorry that I brought my troubles to you," she said in a low voice, miserable and guilty about involving him in her misfortune.

His eyes seared into her. "You think that was your stalker?" His tone was frankly doubting. "How could he find you here? It was a wrong number."

Though she doubted it, she said, "I hope you're right." She stared into the fire, then sighed as the rain came down harder. The day certainly matched her mood. She sighed again and rubbed her arms where chills again ran along her skin.

"Damn," he said and stood.

She stared at him in surprise, then apprehension, as he strode to the sofa, bent and lifted her into his arms.

He returned to the recliner and settled her in his lap, then spread a chenille afghan over both of them. "Relax," he murmured in a gruff but comforting manner.

"I didn't sleep very much last night," she began, then shut up. She didn't want to explain that remark.

With another sigh she laid her head on his shoulder and closed her eyes. Warmth from the fire, the cover and his powerful masculine body seeped into her from all sides.

Feeling safe and cherished and other things she couldn't name, she yawned and did as he had ordered. She fell asleep and hardly roused when he let the chair back into its reclining position.

Clyde opened his eyes, saw that nearly two hours had passed and that the fire had fallen into embers. "Hey," he said softly, hating to wake the woman in his arms.

Her eyes opened at once, looking like twin pieces of a summer sky as she gazed at him.

"The fire is getting low," he said. "I need to add some logs to it."

When she rose, he found he was reluctant to give her up. Her lithe body felt right in his arms. Too right.

"It's time for lunch," she said, also noting the time. "Would you like a sandwich?"

"Yeah, that would be fine."

While she headed for the kitchen, he rebuilt the fire and turned the gas off, which he'd forgotten earlier. The new wood caught fire at once, heating the air that circulated around the firebox and warming the room.

The rain, and sometimes hail, still raged outside. The electricity had flickered on a couple of times, but had promptly gone back off, which wasn't unusual in a Texas thunderstorm. He would hate to be out in it, trying to get the electrical lines back up and working.

Jessica returned, carrying a tray, which she placed on the table beside the recliner. She returned to the kitchen and reappeared with another. Sandwiches, chips, pickles and sliced fruit were on the two plates. Glasses of iced tea accompanied each meal.

"Looks good," he said, every hair on his body rising as electricity radiated between them.

They ate without talking. Her eyes stayed on the fire most of the time. The couple of times their glances met, his blood notched up a few degrees.

The quiet, the intimacy of being inside while the storm swept over the land, the knowledge that they were alone and that the attraction hadn't diminished one bit after that day at the lake burnt through his resolve.

He ate quickly, but food didn't appease his appetite. "Jessica," he said. When she faced him, he couldn't think of another word.

When she averted her gaze and pressed her lips firmly together, he knew she, too, felt the vibes between them.

Setting the tray aside, he stood and paced the narrow

room, restless and irritated with his inability to control the odd need to hold her and claim her as his own. He knew it was a really stupid idea.

Only it wouldn't go away.

When he stopped and stared at her, torn every which way by the hunger and longing he couldn't deny, she shook her head. "We can't," she said breathlessly.

"Can't?" he questioned with a mirthless laugh.

"We shouldn't." She set her tray on the coffee table, the food only half-eaten.

"Tell me to quit breathing," he suggested.

She stood, a tall, slender woman who seemed to match him in every way. He saw the passion in her eyes and his control raveled into shreds.

"Jessica," he said, and this time other words followed. "I can't be with you like this and not want you. But you know that, don't you?"

She gave him a troubled perusal. He couldn't hide the evidence of his hunger for her. "Yes," she said honestly. "It's the same for me. I don't know why…"

Her voice trailed off.

"That part is easy," he said, moving close so that they nearly touched. He wanted to touch her, needed to. "Polar opposites. Male and female. The attraction is as natural as rain." He gestured toward the window. "As sunshine."

He smiled when she did, a tiny smile at the corners of her mouth that indicated humor at their predicament and a worried resignation that it should be so. He realized he understood her as he had no other woman.

"Come with me," he invited huskily.

"Where?"

"My room," he said softly. He took her hand in his. "My bed."

She didn't retreat when he led her toward the doorway.

"My arms," he ended.

Together they went up the stairs. There he found paradise and made sure she found it, too.

Sated, he rested, Jessica secure in his arms, the little frown of worry she'd worn recently smoothed from her lovely, striking face.

He smiled, kissed her and fell into a deep sleep.

Eight

Jessica woke to unusual warmth and comfort. It took her a split second to realize why. She was snuggled against a very strong, very male body. It had been a long time since she'd spent the night with a man.

Five years, she recalled. Five years ago she'd fallen for the marketing director of a cosmetic line. They were shooting the ads along the exotic coasts of the world—Spain, Italy, Turkey, New Zealand and Australia. It had been a magical time.

When they'd returned to the U.S., the magic had disappeared and she'd finally seen him for the egotistical, demanding creature he really was. It had taken several months for this fact to sink in, though. She'd been caught up in a romantic dream of her own making.

And, she admitted, some stubborn part of her hadn't wanted to admit she'd been so terribly wrong.

She sighed and put the memory aside. Clyde was down-to-earth and practical. He acted gruff at times, but he was kind. Also gentle. And the best lover she'd ever had.

After making love in the afternoon, they'd napped, then had soup for dinner and popcorn in the evening. At ten they'd just naturally returned to his bed, made love and slept there, snug in each other's arms. This time he'd had protection and had used it.

She hadn't mentioned her suspicions about the results of their other tryst down by the lake. It was pointless until she was sure. Then she would tell him.

Would he be glad?

"Good morning," he now said in a deep rumble that spoke of contentment and perhaps amusement.

He nibbled on her ear, making her smile. "Hi," she said, then stretched luxuriously.

"The coffee should be ready," he said.

"When did you put it on?"

"About thirty minutes ago while you were still in dreamland. A falling branch woke me. *You* didn't stir a hair."

She laughed. "I can sleep through anything."

"Stay still," he told her when she started to rise. "I'll bring you a cup of coffee."

"Wow, service with a smile."

His smile was enchanting, but his eyes held emotions she couldn't read. He pulled on a sweat suit before leaving the bedroom. Going to her room, she brushed her teeth and rinsed her face, then returned next door.

A few minutes later, Clyde reappeared, this time with a tray holding one plate and two forks. She propped her back against the pillows while he sat on the side of the bed.

It seemed very romantic, sharing the cheese omelet and several slices of toast. When he spread one slice with jelly and held it out to her, she took a bite, then watched as he took the next one.

"It's still raining," she said.

"And windy. It was gusting pretty hard last night. There're several limbs down. I was surprised to find the electricity on this morning. I thought we'd better eat while we had the chance to cook something."

She sipped the hot, delicious coffee. "What do you need to do today?"

"Check the livestock and make sure they're okay. See if Clinton needs any help with the chickens. I'll probably have to replace some shingles on the barn roof, but that'll have to wait until the weather clears."

"Mmm," she said.

"Otherwise," he said with his quiet smile, "we'll have to entertain ourselves as long as it's raining."

"I saw a biography on John Adams I would like to read." She patted back a yawn.

Clyde laughed softly. "Sleepyhead."

"Did we sleep last night?" she asked mock seriously. "I can't seem to remember."

Still chuckling, he removed the tray and disappeared down the hall. She listened to his steps fade as he went down the stairs before she forced herself from the comfortable nest.

She showered and dressed in slacks and a T-shirt, then dried her hair and pulled it into a ponytail. Pausing in front of the mirror, she was surprised by her reflection. She looked young and carefree. Happiness radiated from her like an aura of enchantment.

Some part of her urged caution, but her heart hopped around her chest like a perky robin. Clyde had been her first wild, sweet love. Maybe he was destined to be the last, her one and only true love.

Smiling she went downstairs.

The phone rang just as she entered the kitchen. Clyde's

hands were wet as he washed out the skillet he used for the eggs. "Get that, will you?" he asked.

"Sure." She lifted the receiver. "Flying Aces."

There was silence on the line.

"Hello?" she said.

The hair prickled on her nape as she heard the sound of breathing on the line. She hung up the phone with a bang. Fear and anger jostled for first place in her.

"Who was it?" Clyde asked, finished and drying his hands on the dish towel.

"The stalker."

A beat of silence followed her declaration. "What did he say?" Clyde asked.

"Nothing. Just breathed."

He laid his hands on her shoulders as if to comfort her. "It was a wrong number."

"No."

"It was," he insisted. "He couldn't possibly know where you are. Wrong numbers happen, even in Texas."

It took an effort, but she finally returned his smile. "I think I'll read for a while."

"It's damp and chilly this morning. I'll make a fire, then I'm going outside to check for storm damage." He hesitated. "Don't worry. I won't let anything happen to you. Violet made me promise to keep an eye on you. I wouldn't dare not keep it."

Again she smiled. When he lightly kissed her goodbye after getting the fire blazing in the grate, she resisted the need to cling to him. Instead she settled on the sofa with the thick biography and forced her mind on the words.

After an hour, she laid the book aside and added more logs to the flames. Restless, she roamed from window to window, looking for Clyde. When she spotted him returning from the egg barn, his long stride bringing him to her, she experienced such a dizzy-headed lightness she had to hold on to the windowsill to steady herself.

Mixed concerns warred within. For one, there were the silent phone calls of late, three of them. Three wrong numbers happening in short order, each one hanging up without speaking? She shook her head, not believing it.

Second was the fact that she could be expecting. She had no idea how Clyde would react to this news.

And last but not least—not least at all—was the knowledge that she'd again fallen for the handsome, elusive older brother of the Fortune triplets.

She had no idea where she stood in the grand scheme of his life. Did a mad passion equal a lasting love?

Even bad luck must change eventually, and so it was with the weather. On Thursday, the rain stopped early in the morning and by ten, the sky was clear.

Miles and Clyde had gone to the stock sales near Austin for the day. She had elected to stay at the ranch. Her father liked to attend sales and ranch-related functions just for fun. She would have a hard time explaining why she was in Texas without visiting her parents if her dad spotted her with the Fortune brothers.

Outside she weeded for a couple of hours, then went in to shower and change clothing. Gathering her courage, she admitted it was time to sneak into town and go to the market, which was also the drug store. The need to know if she was pregnant overrode all else.

The old grocery had been taken over by a chain, and since she'd been gone from the area for a long time, she didn't think it likely anyone there would know her.

As a precaution, though, she put her hair up and wore a floppy straw hat along with big sunglasses. In slacks and a plain white T-shirt, she looked like most of the population of the town.

Backing the station wagon out of the neat garage, she realized it felt odd to drive. In the city she didn't bother to own a car. It was too hard to find a parking space, so she used cabs like most sensible residents did.

The two miles to Red Rock zipped by much too fast. She noticed the new houses on the approach to the town, but the town center, with its circular park instead of a square, was the same as she remembered.

The park contained a white gazebo, black wrought-iron posts with lanterns that resembled gaslights with white globes, and lots of benches tucked among shade trees.

Traffic was light and flowed smoothly around the park circle and onto the side streets. Main Street and Sycamore Avenue formed the two major arteries through the obviously booming town. She passed Emma's Café where she and her pals had spent their spare time.

New signs on old offices saddened her as she thought of the attorneys, dentists and doctors she'd once known, fixtures of the town, who had retired or passed away. She didn't recognize many of the new names.

The grocery had been enlarged, taking over the old pool hall that used to be next door, bulldozing the building and turning the area into a parking lot.

"Huh," she muttered, not sure she liked the changes as she pulled into a space and turned off the engine. Pulling her hat down to her eyebrows, she tried to make herself appear shorter as she went inside.

It didn't take long to find the feminine products section and select a pregnancy test kit. She picked up a few other items so the one wouldn't be so conspicuous, paid for them, then hurried outside.

And came face-to-face with her sister.

"Jessica?" Leslie said. "Jessica! It is you!"

"Shh," Jessica hissed. She grabbed Leslie's arm and guided her away from the market's double doors.

Leslie looked completely baffled as they stopped beside the station wagon. "What are you doing here? Are you working? What's going on?"

Jessica smiled wryly at her sister's perfectly natural questions. "How about lunch?" she asked. "Then I'll come clean and explain all."

"You'd better," Leslie said darkly, then spoiled it by laughing. "I thought I was seeing things, but this explains the photo in the paper recently."

Jessica tossed her grocery bag into the station wagon, grateful that her little sis couldn't see the items she'd purchased. The two crossed the street and went into a hole-in-the-wall diner that hadn't been there when she'd lived in the town. "What photo?" Jessica asked.

"In one of those tabloid magazines," Leslie explained. "There was a story about Ryan Fortune at a funeral and how some people think he killed a long-lost relative. I thought it was you in the background of the picture, but I knew it couldn't be. You were presumably a thousand miles away."

Jessica sighed. "I was at the funeral. I suppose it was naive to expect to go unnoticed. Was I identified by the tabloid reporter?"

"No. I recognized Clyde Fortune, who was behind the others as they left the chapel, and then noticed a woman who was with him. My heart nearly jumped right out of my chest, but I thought I must be mistaken in first thinking it was you."

Leslie's eyes questioned Jessica, who nodded, admitting she was the woman clinging to Clyde's arm.

"But what were you doing there? Why are you *here*?"

They were interrupted by a waitress Jessica didn't know and who seemed indifferent to her identity. After she and

Leslie ordered, Leslie called her husband on her cell phone and said she was having lunch with an old friend and that she'd tell him about it later.

"Is it okay if I tell him I saw you?" she asked after punching the off button.

"Yes, but don't tell anyone else." Jessica brought her sister up to date about the stalker.

"You should have come to us," Leslie scolded. "Marty and I would have watched out for you."

Marty was Leslie's husband of almost ten years. High school sweethearts, they had married after graduation and had two wonderful daughters, Douglass and Chanson, both of whom Jessica adored.

"I know," Jessica said, "but I didn't want to put your family, nor our parents, in danger in case this wacko followed me."

"The town has grown so much lately that I don't know everyone anymore, but I haven't seen any strangers, any *suspicious* strangers around," Leslie assured her. "No one's been asking for you that I know of."

"That's a relief."

Leslie gave her big sister a probing study. "So Violet convinced you the Flying Aces would be a safe place?"

Jessica nodded. Her heart beat with a hard thud, impatient to be back on the ranch, to see Clyde and to discover the results of the test kit she'd bought. As much as she loved her sister, she couldn't explain any of these complications at present.

Leslie rolled her eyes, then laughed softly. "If I remember correctly, no place near the Fortune bachelors, either those from Texas or those from New York, was considered safe for young, impressionable females."

"Well, I'm neither young nor impressionable," Jessica said with droll humor.

"Mmm, I think you had a crush on one of the New York cousins once, but I wasn't sure which one."

"Ha," Jessica said, as if this was a ridiculous idea.

"Whatever," Leslie said equably. "It's so good to see you. I didn't realize how much I've missed you until this surprise meeting. Were you going to leave without letting us know? Mom will kill you if you do."

"Actually there's a wedding coming up—"

"Steven Fortune and Amy somebody. He's crazy about her, or so I heard. She's been working with the governor."

"Right. It's at the end of the month. I thought I'd go stay with Mom and Dad after that. I think I'm just paranoid about Roy stalking me."

"You've had no trouble since you arrived?"

Jessica hesitated, then shook her head. "None."

Their food arrived. While they ate, they discussed family happenings. The hardware store was doing more business than they could handle. Marty was thinking of hiring another clerk. The girls, one in third and one in first grade, liked school and their teachers. They were into Girl Scouts and soccer. Both took piano lessons.

"Well, I had better head back to the Flying Aces," Jessica said after almost two hours had passed.

Leslie grimaced, but walked her back to the station wagon. "Promise you'll spend a couple of days with us after you visit with the folks."

"I promise." Jessica signed a cross over her heart.

When she drove off, she looked back and waved while her sister stared after the departing vehicle. Leslie waved, then hurried down the street to the hardware store to share her news with Marty.

Of all the dumb luck, Jessica mused on the short trip to the ranch. Running into Leslie on the street. Still, she'd been glad to see her sister.

To heck with the stalker. Other than those phone calls, which probably were wrong numbers, she'd had no trouble. Roy was most likely obsessed with some other woman by now.

No one was at the house when she arrived. Quickly she ran inside and up the staircase to her room. When the test was completed, she considered the results in puzzlement.

She'd been so sure…but now…well, she wasn't sure at all. How accurate were these tests anyway?

Perhaps she should wait a couple of days and try it again, although according to the instructions, this should have been plenty of time for a positive result.

If she were pregnant. Which she didn't seem to be.

She tossed the stick into the trash basket along with the box and wrappings, oddly disappointed.

The crowd pushed forward as soon as the gates were opened. Clyde apologized when he jostled an older man also heading for a row of ringside seats inside the covered stock-sale arena.

"That's all right," the man answered, glancing at him with bright blue eyes and a friendly smile.

Clyde's lungs seized up for a second. Jessica's father. She'd said the older man liked to attend the sales, but he hadn't thought once of actually running into him.

"You're two of the Fortune triplets," Mr. Miller said, including Miles in his glance, "but I can't tell which two you are."

"I'm Clyde, Mr. Miller," he said as he shook hands. "And this is Miles. Steven is the absent one. He couldn't be with us today."

"Actually he wasn't invited," Miles interjected. "We're here to buy him a surprise bull for his new ranch."

Mr. Miller appeared thoughtful. "Steven is the one marrying that gal who plans some of the governor's events, right?"

"Right," Clyde affirmed.

"I saw the announcement in the paper. Bet that will be a big to-do. Which one of you is going to be his best man?"

Miles answered. "I think Ryan Fortune is doing the honors for Steven. The plan is for a small family wedding at present, but I suppose that can change at any time. These things tend to grow, it seems."

"Don't I know it!" Mr. Miller said. "By the time my younger daughter got married, everybody in Red Rock was at the wedding."

The three men chuckled in complete understanding as they chose seats in the first row so they could closely inspect the livestock brought into the arena.

"The bull is our wedding present for Steven," Miles said, "but I'm not sure if it's appropriate for Amy. I think we should get her something for the house. Maybe your daughter can advise us on that."

Clyde gave his brother a hard poke in the ribs. Miles glared, then realization dawned in his eyes as he recalled that Jessica's visit was unknown to her family.

"Leslie knows about things like that," Mr. Miller said, nodding. "She's added a gift department to the hardware store. It seems to be doing well."

Clyde sat between his brother and Jessica's father to waylay further conversation.

"Sorry," Miles muttered.

He smiled slightly, acknowledging that Jessica's dad hadn't caught on to which daughter his brother had meant.

For some reason, a wave of guilt sluiced over Clyde like the first spray of hot water when he stepped into the shower. Even if the older man had known of Jessica's visit, he wouldn't know that she had spent the previous night in his arms.

Another type of heat rushed through him. Jessica. Those long, slender legs, delicate but strong. The wonder of her body, filled with feminine delights. She'd certainly delighted him beyond anything he'd ever experienced.

His head grew dizzy as blood pounded through him. He cleared his mind with an effort.

"You heard from your sister lately?" Mr. Miller asked.

Clyde and Miles glanced at each other, then away. So his brother had caught the undertones in the older man's voice, too. Miles pretended to be interested in the sales brochure, leaving Clyde to answer.

"Uh, a few weeks ago. She's on a cruise this month."

"Mmm," Mr. Miller said. "Jessica hasn't called in a while, but she would tell her mother if she were going on a long trip. She didn't answer her phone last weekend and her cell phone isn't working. We get a recording that says it's disconnected, but it must out of order. I'm not worried, but you know how women get in a fret about things."

"Uh, perhaps she'll call soon," Clyde suggested. He would see that she did. Her father was clearly concerned, despite his denial. Jessica would feel bad about worrying her parents when he told her of the conversation.

An impatience to be home took hold of him. It lasted throughout the morning, during lunch with the other two, and into the afternoon when he and Miles bid on and purchased the prize bull they'd decided on as a present for their brother's nuptials.

After saying goodbye to Mr. Miller, Clyde arranged for the delivery of the bull to the new ranch. Miles had decided to stay in Austin and visit with old friends they'd met as they left the stock sale.

"I may stay the weekend," he'd said upon parting.

Clyde wondered what woman, or women, his brother would call to fill those long hours. Miles, with a reputation as a playboy, had plenty of choices.

For himself, Clyde preferred the solitary life. He firmly reiterated this fact to himself on the ninety-mile drive back to the Flying Aces spread. The sun was sinking below the horizon by the time he arrived.

The front yard had been weeded, he noted, stopping near the barn and stable area. Lights were on inside the house, and he could see Jessica moving about the kitchen, going from the stove to the refrigerator and back.

His heart kicked up its speed.

Danger. He felt the word echo inside him, a warning that he was becoming too involved, too susceptible to the charms of the woman in his house.

After turning off the engine, he sat there in the truck for a moment, as if to get up his courage to go inside. At the same time he couldn't deny the need to rush in and enclose her in his arms, to grab her to him and experience the reality of her body against his, to have the fact reaffirmed that she welcomed his embrace.

He muttered an imprecation and wondered where this was all leading. Nowhere, came the answer from that cynical part of him that had learned the lying ways of the world, and women in particular, at the ripe old age of twenty-two. He was no longer the young man who'd believed in love and all the trappings that passion inspired.

Both reluctant and eager, he shook his head cynically and strode to the house through the long, silent shadows of twilight. He and Jessica were adults. They each knew how the world turned. There were no false expectations on either side.

"Well, hello," she said, smiling when he entered the back door. "You're just in time. Have you eaten?"

"No."

"I prepared a shepherd's pie, if you would like to join me. Did you and Miles get the bull you wanted?"

"Yes." He hung his hat on a peg near the door. Sticking his hands in his back pockets, he leaned against the counter while she finished preparing a salad.

The aroma of food filled the kitchen, the scent coming from the oven. When she opened the door and removed a casserole, he saw the mashed potatoes on top were browned a crisp golden color all over. The beef and vegetables bubbled in a rich gravy in the middle of the dish.

Hunger overcame the troubled thoughts that had plagued him on the trip home, hunger for food, for her, for things that didn't last.

Sucking in a harsh breath, he told her, "Miles and I ran into your father at the stock sale."

"Oh, no," she said, her eyes going wide. "Did he say anything? Did he see our picture in the tabloid?"

"Whoa," Clyde said. "What picture?"

She told him of going to town and running into her sister and them having lunch together. "I had to tell her what was going on."

"I guess the secret is out, then," he murmured. "Your father doesn't yet know you're here. We didn't mention it. However, he is worried. Apparently your mother tried to call you last weekend and couldn't get an answer. They think your cell phone isn't working."

"I need to call them." She placed the shepherd's pie on the granite counter of the island, added plates, silverware, napkins and salad bowls filled with fresh greens. "Iced tea?" she asked.

"Please."

He took his usual place at the end while she did the same. When she finished helping herself to the food, he scooped a big portion onto his plate. He studied the scene from a distance, as if he were observing the couple from a point high on the ceiling.

They ate the delicious dinner and chatted about her father and the livestock auction, about ranching and its rewards and hardships.

"Being here this month has reminded me of how much I love this country. I guess Dorothy was right—there's no place like home."

"Yes," he said huskily, finishing the meal.

Had she really been there a month? Almost, he realized. The next Friday would be the last day of the month.

Steven's wedding day.

The full impact of his triplet's marriage hit him then. His brother would be a family man. It was almost mind-boggling.

His brain filled with swirling images of home and family, a wife and children, things he'd always assumed would one day be his.

"I found ice cream in the freezer. Would you like some with sliced bananas and chocolate sauce?" she asked.

"No," he said. Without thinking, he reached for her. "The only thing I want is you."

He kissed the startled smile from her lips.

Nine

Jessica returned to the family room where Clyde lounged on the sofa while watching a football game. He lifted one arm and held her against his side when she accepted the tacit invitation to sit beside him.

"Are your folks okay?" he asked.

"Yes. Dad mentioned seeing you and Miles at the auction today. He said you both had grown into nice young men."

Clyde grinned. "I'm sure he had his doubts about us when we visited the Double Crown each summer."

"I don't know," she said in a musing tone. "However, he did say that he would lock me up the whole time you boys were in town if he ever caught me seeing one of you."

Clyde's eyebrows shot up. "Really?"

"No." She laughed and snuggled close. "You older men didn't look at your sister's friend once, much less twice."

"We were blind in those days," he murmured.

"Nope. I was a shy, awkward kid, hardly 'date bait,' as the local boys so elegantly put it."

"But now you're striking," he said in teasing tones.

He turned her face up to his and kissed her lightly on the mouth. An hour ago he'd turned her world upside-down while he'd kissed her deeply and passionately as they'd made love. They'd acted as if it had been days instead of hours since they'd last touched each other.

Making love with him had been very satisfying. Being with him like this—like an old married couple, content to be together—was also satisfying.

Perhaps it should be terrifying, she admitted. Each hour together drew her deeper into a relationship that might not be wise.

Whatever the future, she was content. Clyde was an honorable man. He wouldn't abandon his child, nor its mother. Everything about him indicated his deep, caring nature. There were feelings between them.

When the football game was over, he flipped the channel to a news station. The weather was supposed to be partly cloudy over the weekend with a chance of thunderstorms late in the afternoon tomorrow and on Saturday. Sunday should be a fair day with scattered clouds.

"What do you have to do this weekend?" she asked.

"Cull the cows we're going to sell. The truck will pick them up on Saturday. Miles volunteered to follow them to Houston for the big auction there."

"How do you know which ones you want to sell?"

"I track each cow in the computer. The ones that stop producing have to make way for the new breeding cows."

"So scientific," she said, more to herself than him. She was thinking of the test she'd taken earlier. Was she breeding or not? The test said no, but she was still late.

"A rancher has to be on top of the latest info," he told

her. "The financial margins are so narrow, one wrong decision could wipe out a year's profits."

She thought of all the money she made just to wear the latest fashions and smile at the camera. Her personal lifestyle was conservative, so she'd managed to save most of what she'd made for the past ten years.

"I've been lucky," she said.

"Lucky?"

"That I happened to be at the right place at the right time when Sondra came to visit her niece, that she spotted me and offered to represent me—"

"For a hefty cut of all you made," he interjected. "Violet says you worked hard to get where you are."

"My trials and tribulations were nothing compared to hers. I don't see how anyone makes it through medical training. I worried about her during her internship."

"She loves her career."

"Yes, but it's been difficult, more so of late," Jessica said. "I think we're both ready for a change."

"Which is why she's on a cruise, I suppose."

"Yes. She's rethinking her life."

"Are you really contemplating giving up the glamorous career and returning to Texas?" he asked.

She nodded against his shoulder. "I'm signed up for two more years of haute couture work. At present, Sondra is negotiating a three-year contract with a cosmetics company. If I take it, I'll do only their ads and will travel some as their spokesperson. It would be a good way to taper off, then retire gracefully. By then, I hope to have a couple of kids and the usual assortment of dogs and cats."

"What about a husband? Does he figure into your equation for the good life?"

"Of course. I want my children to have a full-time father as well as a mother." She paused, then asked, "What about you? What's in your future?"

He shrugged, his eyes going dark and moody as if he gazed into a distant, painful place. "Steven and Amy can take care of producing the grandchildren my mom wants. Miles will probably marry someday. That lets me off the hook."

"You were engaged once. I was told she died." Jessica realized where her thoughts were taking her and shut up. She didn't want to arouse sad memories.

"She left me standing at the altar," he corrected in cynical amusement. "Not literally, but almost. She didn't show up at the meeting place so we could go to the justice of the peace and get hitched. I waited for hours, a big bouquet of red roses wilting in my hands."

Jessica was shocked. She couldn't imagine any woman running out on one of the Fortune triplets.

"I told my family she died in a car accident," he finished, his face set and without expression.

She sensed the uncertainty he'd gone through, then the pain when he'd realized the woman wasn't going to show up for the wedding. Humiliated, he'd returned home alone to face his family's expectations.

She ran her fingers along his jaw in a gentle caress. "She broke your heart," she said huskily.

"Do you feel sorry for me?" he mocked.

"For that young man. He was sincere and honest."

"He was stupid," he corrected. "She did me a favor, actually. Claudia pretended to be pregnant by some guy who'd deserted her. Sucker that I was, I gave her money. She took it and left town. That cured me of my romantic illusions."

"You were generous. I can't believe how unselfish, how caring you were." Jessica couldn't help the emotion in her eyes and the slight tremor in her voice. She gazed at him with admiration and love.

Tell him, some foolish, hopeful part of her urged. *Tell him there may be a child, one that is his.*

But she couldn't quite get the words to form. She had her own uncertainties about how he would take the news.

A muscle moved in his jaw. He smoothed the frown from her face with a finger along her forehead. "Don't set me up as a romantic hero in your mind. I'm not that boy. I'm not lonely or plagued by regret. My life is just the way I want it. That's how it's going to stay."

"I see."

"Do you?" he questioned.

There was a hardness in him now that closed the subject to further discussion. She fell silent, content for the moment to simply be with him, here in the soft quiet of the house, just the two of them.

"Ready for bed?" he asked.

"Yes."

Going with him up the steps, she decided she would get another test kit and check it again before telling him anything. There was plenty of time to think about the future.

About nine months.

She smothered a laugh as excitement tumbled through her like acrobats doing tricks on a high wire at a circus.

Her, a mom!

Clyde kept an eye on Jessica the next morning. Like him, she was working with the cattle. He had her sitting on the fence, swinging the two gates as needed. Her face was flushed and her eyes sparkled as she helped him with the chore. She seemed to be enjoying herself.

Smiling, he countered as a queen cow challenged him and his mount. The experienced cutting horse quickly headed off the cow and forced it back into the milling herd.

He checked ear tags and directed those to be sold

through the chute and into a pen for pickup by the big cattle truck in the morning. The others he guided into the adjoining pasture where they settled to grazing.

"Chute," he called, herding another group of three toward his helper.

Jessica quickly closed the gate to block the pasture entrance and force the cows the other way.

Once in the narrow fenced chute, the cows couldn't turn around and so had no choice but to go into the holding pen beside the barn.

Jessica laughed aloud as she swung the gates the opposite way when he called out, "Pasture," to indicate the cattle they were keeping. The cows appeared confused by the change, but obediently went through into the pasture.

For a second he let himself observe her while images of them rolled through his mind like an old-fashioned movie—him and her making a life for themselves in the Wild West of yore, working together, facing danger….

Tenderness welled up inside, causing him to swallow hard as he tried to suppress it. He warned himself about being a fool for a woman, but try as he might, he couldn't find any cracks or flaws in her character.

She was what she was—a country girl who'd made good and was proud of it, but not conceited.

He liked her down-to-earth practicality about her life, her career and herself. Ah, but there had to be a hidden quirk that he hadn't yet detected. No one was as perfect as she was…or pretended to be.

She liked the wide-open spaces of the ranch. She liked working, whether before a camera or herding cattle or washing and sorting eggs. Clinton and his wife and kids sang her praises every moment he was around them.

So did Violet. She'd talked about her friend and her many virtues for years.

Suspicion reared its head. Had his dear sister and Jessica planned this? Did they think he was lonely and ripe to be lured into marriage and all that?

With a model who flew all over the world and met the crowned heads of royalty in her travels?

No way. At this moment, she had some bug in her ear about settling down to marriage and kids, but that was the old biological clock ticking. She was getting old for a model, she'd said, so maybe she'd decided on a new career—wife and mom and country living.

Fine. But he wasn't going to be the all-American husband and father in her dream world.

Nope, she could just find another gullible stud for the offspring she professed to want. The marriage wouldn't last five years, and then there would be the complications of divorce and custody of the children.

If he ever had kids, he wanted them to live at the ranch all year, not just summers and holidays. He intended to raise his family, and he wanted a wife who would be there at his side through thick and thin and all that.

Jessica would soon miss the glamorous life, the travel and privileges of being part of the world's elite set. No matter how much in love a couple were when they said their vows, family life could wear thin when problems came up.

Anger surged through him as he thought of all the problems that would ensue if he was crazy enough to get more involved with her. He frowned impatiently as his emotions went through more ups and downs than a Texas road in the hill country.

What had happened to the placid life he'd had just a month ago? *Her,* he answered his own question.

He studied her lithe elegance while she waved the breeding herd through the gate into the pasture and the others into the sales pen. His heart clenched up as if a giant fist had taken hold of it and was squeezing out the last drop of blood.

With a curse, he finished sorting the last of the cattle, told her to close the gates, then reined the horse close to the fence. "Hop on," he invited.

She swung a leg over the saddle behind him without the least hesitation and wrapped her arms around his waist. "Mmm, that was fun."

"Yeah, right." But he laughed when she did.

He headed for the stable to unsaddle and turn the cow pony out to pasture, too. While her body felt great against his back, her small, firm breasts caressing him, he determined not to get caught up in the dream of thinking she was his in any permanent way.

After all, the reality of sleeping with her was pretty exciting, and it was enough. He didn't need more. Satisfied that he'd figured out all the emotional kinks, he finished the chores while she watched, then went to the house.

The phone was ringing when they entered. Glancing at the clock, he saw it was already one. No wonder he was starving.

"Hello," he said.

"It's Steven," his brother said. "Do you want company tonight?"

"Like who?" he asked.

"Me and Amy. I thought we might come out and grill some steaks and chat for a while."

"Sure. It's your place, too, although we rarely see you anymore," Clyde added.

"Are you trying to put a guilt trip on me?" Steven demanded, not at all bothered.

"What good would that do? You're so far up in the stars, you don't notice mundane, earthly things anymore, like the cattle sale in Houston."

"Miles said he was taking the cattle in."

"That's right. Jessica helped me finish the sorting this morning. We're ready to roll when the truck gets here."

"Good. I was wondering if you and Miles wanted to buy out my share since I have the new ranch to run. Think about it," Steven advised before Clyde could respond.

Actually he'd already wondered if Steven wanted to sell his share since he had a full plate with his Austin properties. "Sure. See you later."

"Around six?"

"That'll be fine." When he hung up, Clyde glanced at Jessica, who was pouring them each a tall glass of tea with lots of ice. "Steven and Amy are coming out for dinner. I'll grill some steaks."

"Great. There's plenty of stuff for salad. We can have baked potatoes and asparagus, too. And Cimma still has tomatoes in her garden. She said to help ourselves. How about lunch? Do you want a ham sandwich? Or how about grilled chicken salad? I like those."

"The chicken salad sounds good. I don't think I've ever had one grilled."

He took a long drink of the iced tea before scouting out the corn chips in the pantry. He set those on the counter along with the salsa and a jar of peppers. They worked in unison as if they'd been doing this for ages.

A man could get used to having a beautiful woman around, he admitted. He frowned, but the stubborn thought wouldn't disappear from his head.

"How are the wedding plans going?" Jessica asked Amy that evening after the greetings were over.

"I'm not sure," she admitted with a rueful smile.

"She's a nervous wreck," Steven interjected.

Amy sighed. "I thought it was difficult to plan the governor's function for Ryan Fortune, but everyone knew the date for that and that it couldn't be changed. Our wedding is like a Ping-Pong ball, hopping back and forth according to the governor's schedule, Ryan's schedule, Steven's parents' schedule…and the schedule of the police working on Christopher Jamison's mysterious death."

Clyde passed around glasses of wine, then the four went out on the patio to relax before finishing the preparations for dinner. Jessica had already set out platters of chips and two dips, one made with cheese, one with salsa. The couples helped themselves to the appetizers.

"Don't tell me they still suspect Ryan," Clyde said in obvious disgust of the officials' ineptitude, taking a seat beside Jessica at the patio table.

Steven shrugged. "If so, they don't have enough evidence to arrest him."

"They should concentrate on finding the real murderer," Clyde stated.

"I totally agree," Steven said.

Jessica realized the two brothers were not only defensive on Ryan's behalf, but there was a genuine closeness between the men and their older relative.

That was to be expected, she mused. The triplets had spent a lot of time at the Double Crown while growing up. The fact that they'd chosen to live nearby spoke of strong family ties. She liked that fact about them. It indicated they would form lasting bonds within their own families.

Her gaze settled on Clyde as warmth spread from her heart to every part of her. He was wonderful in so many ways it made her giddy to recount them. Every day she was falling more and more in love with this strong, serious man.

Happiness echoed through her innermost being. It was so compelling she knew she was going to have to tell him her news soon or burst from the effort of holding it in. In spite of the test kit, she was almost positive she was expecting. Her monthlies were very regular....

"What?" she asked, suddenly aware that the other three were looking at her.

"Shall I put the steaks on now?" Clyde asked.

"Whenever you're ready. The asparagus and dinner rolls will only take five minutes, and the potatoes are done."

"May I help you do something?" Amy asked.

"Sure. I was thinking we could eat out here?" She shot a questioning glance at Clyde.

He nodded. "I haven't seen any mosquitoes, so we should be okay. We can go in later if we have to."

Amy accompanied Jessica into the house. "Bowls are on the counter over there. The salad is in the refrigerator. That's the dressing." Jessica pointed out the items while she arranged different kinds of bread in a wooden bowl.

"Have you enjoyed your visit?" the other woman asked. "Steven said you were returning to New York soon."

"It's been a lovely, relaxing time," Jessica affirmed. "But all vacations come to an end. I'll visit my family for a few days before returning to the city."

"But you are coming to the wedding, right?"

Jessica nodded.

Amy finished dividing the salad among the bowls after tossing it with the dressing. She laughed softly. "I still can't believe Steven and I will be married next week. Thursday is only six days away."

"Is your new home ready?"

"Just about. Most of the furniture is in. Pictures and things like that can wait." Amy gestured toward the office across the wide foyer and the flowers in assorted containers in the kitchen and on the formal dining room table. "You've done quite a bit here. I've never seen the house looking so warm and inviting."

"It's a lovely place, isn't it? Finding the shed filled with furniture was like stumbling upon a secret treasure. There's an old Victorian love seat I'm going to reupholster before I leave."

"Clyde should give it to you as a thank-you for all the work you've done in setting up the office."

An idea came to Jessica. "You should see if there's anything you can use in your new home. I saw a small table with a lyre base. The marble top was broken, but that can easily be replaced, if you're interested in something like that."

"I am. We're still looking for a table to go in the entrance foyer. An antique piece would be perfect. You would have to extend your visit so you can show me how to refinish it," Amy said with a sly glance and a definite twinkle in her eyes.

Jessica grinned. "Do I detect a matchmaking gleam in that innocent expression?"

Amy only smiled and looked wise.

"You and Violet," Jessica said and rolled her eyes. "She's been trying to hook me up with one of her brothers for the past five years. She was very disappointed that Jack and I didn't take one look and fall head over heels for each other. She nearly browbeat us for not cooperating."

When Amy didn't answer, Jessica glanced around. The two men stood at the door. "I've come for the steaks," Clyde said, a tightness in his expression that hadn't been there earlier.

"And I've come to refill the wineglasses," Steven announced. He refilled his glass, then his brother's.

"I thought we would start on the salads while the steaks cook," Jessica said to Clyde.

He nodded, lifted the platter of meat and headed for the patio again. Steven followed.

Amy smothered a laugh. "He's jealous," she said. "The

Fortune triplets have hard shells, but they're soft as butter once you get inside. Clyde locked his heart after his fiancée died, but it's time he opened up again."

Jessica thought so, too, but for different reasons.

Overall, Clyde thought the evening had gone well. Jessica seemed to hit it off with Steven and Amy. But then she seemed to hit it off with everybody she met.

A flush of emotion startled him. He realized he was proud of her and the way she made others comfortable in his home. The house displayed all the feminine touches his mother introduced when she was there—flowers and baskets with dried grasses and pine cones, candles on the table.

The meal had been delicious, too. The dressing on the salad had been made by her.

There didn't appear to be anything she couldn't do. He wasn't sure if this pleased him or put him on the defensive. He couldn't even figure out why it mattered that he figure out an answer to his confused emotions.

Hearing the water come on upstairs, he stopped the circling thoughts, locked the doors and hurried up the steps. Jessica's door was open. He paused on the threshold and took in the room.

Everything in it spoke of her. The John Adams biography was on the bedside table. A pair of reading glasses rested on top of it. Hmm, he hadn't seen her wearing those. A single rose was in a bud vase. A sweater was tossed on the back of the chair next to the windows.

Inhaling deeply, he drew her scent into his being. She liked light floral fragrances. So did he, he'd discovered since they'd become lovers.

Lovers.

The very intimacy of the word painted passion-laden pictures in his mind of the way they touched each other.

Sometimes after making love, he simply liked to look at her and run his fingertips over her silky skin.

He'd learned a lot about her in the past few days. Where her tickle spot was. The way she liked to be caressed. When she was near the height of passion. He wondered what it would be like to live with her for a long time....

Realizing where his mind, already hazy with desire, was leading him, he cut the thought, and headed for the open door of the bathroom.

She smiled at him, then continued brushing her teeth. The blue nightgown shimmered as she moved, compelling him to move closer, to touch.

Ah, coolness, then the warmth of her body through the silk. He rested his hands at her hips, liking the tactile sensations, the sweet scent of her underlying the minty flavor in the toothpaste. He knew the taste of her, the feel, the aroma...the essence of her as a woman.

Unable to resist, he leaned forward and laid a hundred quick kisses on the back of her neck.

"No fair," she spluttered. After rinsing her toothbrush and mouth, she quickly dried her hands and face, then turned to him. "A real kiss," she demanded.

He delighted in doing as ordered.

The kiss was long and deep. It heated the blood and sent a swift hard arousal into his lower regions. She brushed against him experimentally, then with a little urgent moan, more forcibly.

"It's good to be wanted," he murmured, kissing across her cheek to her ear and nibbling on the delicate lobe.

"It's overwhelming...to want this way...to feel as if...you're going to explode." She kissed him at every little pause, then nipped along his neck.

"Yes," he agreed, his voice thick and strained as desire drummed through him. "You make me dizzy."

Her soft laughter sang through him like the sweet notes of a violin played by a master. "My knees are getting weak," she warned, leaning into his embrace.

He could identify with that. Making love with her did all kinds of strange things to him. Lifting her, he carried her to the bed and, with a caveman growl, tossed her onto it and fell on top, catching himself on his knees and elbows so he wouldn't crush her slender form with his greater weight.

To him, she seemed fragile and delicate. He felt strong and protective in response. The emotion felt right...so right...so very right.

They made love with the intensity of those still new to each other, yet familiar enough to be comfortable in the knowledge of what each of them liked.

After a long while, when neither could hold out another second, he secured protection, then came to her in one slow, satisfying thrust. Like his most precious possession, he explored her with care and gentleness, then with greater force as she indicated she wanted more.

At last he gave in to her demands and moved to her rhythm, letting the tidal wave of need overtake them.

"Yes, yes, yes," she said in a fierce whisper, then gave a whimper and held her breath as the climax caught her in its passionate upheaval.

He let himself go with her.

The contentment was as pleasurable in the aftermath as the buildup and appeasement of hunger had been during their lovemaking. It was a long time before he could move.

After hours or eons—he couldn't say which—he unwrapped himself from their sleepy embrace and went into the bathroom. As he disposed of the condom, his attention was caught by a word on the box in the trash can.

Pregnancy.

Lifting the box, he read the information on it. He stared at the words while his brain tried to make sense of them. It was no use.

Pregnancy. Test. Kit.

The words sank into his stunned mind. A pregnancy test kit. In Jessica's bathroom. He felt as if he'd been sucker punched right in the gut.

He strode into the bedroom and stopped beside the bed. When she opened her eyes and smiled at him, he held the box so she could see it.

"What is this?" he asked in a very quiet, very controlled voice.

Ten

Jessica, warm and content, reluctantly opened her eyes. They widened of their own volition when she recognized the box Clyde held. "Oh, that," she murmured, feeling both shy and excited at telling him her suspicions.

"Yeah, this," he said, crossing the room and taking a seat on the edge of the bed.

He tossed the box on the mattress, where it tumbled several times before coming to rest a few inches from her. She picked it up, gave him a rueful smile, then placed the empty container on the bedside table.

"Well," she began, "after that afternoon at the lake, I, uh, thought I could be expecting. We didn't, uh…"

"Have any protection," he stated bluntly, his eyes never leaving her face.

"Yes. Later, when I realized I was late, I went into Red Rock and bought the test kit. That was the day I ran into my sister and learned our picture had been in a national tabloid." She glanced at him to make sure he recalled the day.

He nodded. Her heart plunged at the grimness of his expression. "Are you pregnant?" he asked.

"I don't know."

His eyes narrowed as he studied her like he would shake the truth out if she didn't confess all.

"The test was negative," she explained, gesturing toward the test kit.

He apparently heard the uncertainty in her voice. "But?" he questioned.

"But I'm still late."

He blinked once as he took in this news, then he stared out the window at the night-shrouded sky. Finally he sighed and turned back to her. "Tell me the truth," he said quietly. "Did you and Violet plan this?"

She shook her head adamantly. "No, never."

He was silent for a long moment. Jessica held her tongue, too. He would either believe her or he wouldn't. From the set of his jaw, she was pretty sure she knew the answer. He laughed, a brief sound with no trace of humor.

"All right," he said, but doubtfully.

Pushing herself upright against the pillows, she met his eyes without flinching. "I'm not your former fiancée," she told him in a low, fierce voice, her temper rising at his obvious suspicions of her motives. "I'm not after your money. I have plenty of my own."

"You said Violet had been trying to hook you up with Jack or one of us for years," he reminded her.

A shiver ran down her back at his icy tone. She managed a wry laugh. "Your sister is a very dear friend, but her romantic schemes are not mine."

He ran a hand around the back of his neck as if an ache gathered there, and gave her a keen but uncertain perusal.

"Whether you believe me or not is something you'll have to figure out for yourself," she told him. "I honestly don't know if there may be a baby. If so, you don't have to worry. I won't ask anything of you—"

She blinked as he came toward her, his face inches from her, fury in the black depths of his eyes. "Any child of mine will be raised by me. That's a truth you can take to the bank. I would never run out on a kid."

"I would never deprive a child of its father," she said just as fiercely. "If he sincerely wants to take part for love of the child and not revenge on its mother."

He bolted upright as if she'd slapped him. "Is that the kind of man you think I am? If so, I'm surprised you would choose me for father material."

"Oh, for heaven's sake!" She threw the sheet back, climbed out of the cozy bed and paced the floor, pulling on the blue robe with self-conscious dignity. "I didn't *choose* anything. I didn't plan that episode at the lake. It was as spontaneous on my part as yours. Do you think only men lose their heads in the heat of the moment? Believe me, I must have been out of my mind to think that I…that we…"

He yanked on his underwear and jeans, leaving the latter unfastened, which she found alarmingly sexy, and faced her, arms cocked at his sides like a gunslinger of old ready to draw his pistols.

"That we what?" he demanded.

"That we were falling in love." She rolled her eyes at the stark absurdity of the idea. "Don't worry. I'm cured of that notion."

"You don't pull any punches, do you?"

The question was rhetorical, but she said, "I'm trying to be honest with you."

He thought it over, then nodded as if he'd decided to believe her. "Okay, I'll give you that."

She refrained from a snide thanks for his forbearance.

Pacing to the window, he stared into the darkness. "The question is, what do we do now?"

"We wait."

"Wait?"

"To see if I'm expecting or just overanxious." She managed a smile. "I've never found myself in this situation before. It makes a person a tad—"

She couldn't think of a simple word to describe the wonder and worry, the excitement and apprehension, the total uncertainty and joy of possible parenthood.

He heaved a sigh. "Yeah, I get the picture." He paced some more, then stopped in front of her. "Look, we're in this together. I'll take responsibility for my part."

"How noble," she murmured.

Ignoring her, he rubbed the back of his neck. "There's a saying—'Give me a child until he's seven and he's mine for life.' If we agreed to stay in the marriage that long, the kid would have a good start."

She waited silently while he planned their future, her heartbeat a dull thump that echoed through her whole body.

"Most marriages that make it through the first year last around ten years. I read that somewhere," he told her, so earnest she almost smiled.

She nodded instead.

"You seem to fit in here at the ranch. Cimma and her daughter will help me out with the baby when you have to go to a photo shoot or whatever." He thought it over. "We can pick up a license Monday and get married right away."

"No," she said when he paused and looked her way.

"Why not?"

"First, we don't know if there is a child, so any marriage plans would be premature."

His sudden smile caused her heart to lurch. "I think,"

he murmured, "we can assume there is. We're too potent together not to have results."

A flush spread from her chest to her neck to her face and ears. Soon heat radiated in hot waves from her body.

He touched her cheek. "There are worse things," he said with an arrogant smile.

Pushing his hand away, she paced the room. Finally she shook her head. "It wouldn't work. Let's take it one day at a time until we know what's what."

He strode to the door, clearly impatient with her hesitation. "If there's a child, I will be a part of its life. A large part," he stated.

Giving her a meaningful glance that was full of warning about the consequences if she should try to deceive him, he left the room. She heard him go next door, then the soft sound of his bedroom door closing behind him.

"So will I," she said into the silence. Sinking onto the bed, she laid a hand on her abdomen and wondered exactly what fate had in store for them.

Clyde watched while Miles used the end of a rope to keep the cattle moving up the loading chute and into the truck that would take them to the big auction. When the beasts were inside, he helped the trucker close the door and fasten it securely for the trip to Houston.

He and the trucker agreed on the count, which matched the number on the computerized list. After signing the bill of lading, he headed across the cattle pen.

"I'll be back tomorrow night," Miles told him.

Clyde nodded, checked the gate to the holding pen, then yawned. "What time is it?"

"A little after eight," Miles told him. "Didn't you sleep well last night?"

Clyde grimaced. "I slept okay."

"I thought Jessica looked tired this morning," his brother continued when Clyde said nothing more. "What's happened between you two?"

Clyde shot his triplet a warning glance. He wasn't in the mood to discuss Jessica.

"Come on," Miles drawled. "Even a blind man could sense the sparkle between you two. Now it's gone. Did you have a lover's quarrel?"

Clyde realized Miles wasn't going to be satisfied until he had the whole of it. Except he wasn't going to disclose that much. "Sort of."

"What about?"

Clyde muttered an expletive. "I didn't realize you were so meddlesome."

Miles shrugged. "I'm worried about Jessica. She came down here to get away from one obsessive guy. It hardly seems fair to have her heart broken by another."

"Her heart isn't broken," Clyde informed his nosy sibling. "Don't you need to get on the road?"

Miles ignored the suggestion. "So what's the problem?"

Clyde headed for the house. "I have paperwork to catch up on," he said. "There's no problem."

Miles grabbed his arm, stopping him before they reached the back door. "I think there is. The light has gone out of Jessica. She's sad. And trying to hide it."

Pulling away from his brother's grasp, Clyde tried to deny any part in their guest's woes. He sighed instead. "She may be pregnant," he stated bluntly.

A surprised grin broke over Miles's face. "Hey, that's great! So when is the wedding?"

"There's no rush. We're waiting to be sure."

"You want to marry her, right?"

"Does it matter?" Clyde demanded. "Women put things into motion, then expect men to put them right."

Anger lodged in his sibling's eyes, tightening the line of his jaw. Clyde could feel the harsh tension in his own face as eyes very much like his own stared at him.

Miles glanced in the kitchen window as if checking for Jessica. "You're a fool if you don't snatch her up," he said in a low tone so his voice wouldn't carry.

"And then what? Happily ever after? Yeah, right."

"Don't let what happened to you years ago ruin your chances at happiness now," Miles advised.

"What do you know about it?" Clyde asked in a snarl, irritated with the whole conversation and with his brother for persisting in something that wasn't his business.

"There was no accident on the day you were supposed to pick up Claudia. No one died. Steven and I checked the newspaper. We think she stood you up. We wondered if you gave her money and she took off."

Clyde glared at his brother.

"Ah, I see you did."

Clyde shrugged. "I was a sucker for a hard-luck story. I'm not that stupid now. I hope," he added, forcing a wry grin. "You and Steven never said anything."

"It was your business. So is the situation between you and Jessica, but I'm going to butt in, anyway."

Clyde didn't want any helpful advice, but he kept his mouth shut and waited for his brother to get it out of his system.

"Don't let a good thing get away because of past hurts," Miles said with great sagacity. "Jessica is a square dealer. She doesn't need your money, so anything she feels for you must be real."

"If only it were that simple," Clyde muttered.

"Why isn't it?"

"Because."

"Because why?" Miles asked, the usual amusement returning to his eyes as he needled his triplet.

Clyde held his temper with an effort. "She's feeling the pinch of time, that's all. So what happens five years down the road when she's tired and bored with kids and ranch life and all that? What happens then?"

Miles walked over to the door and paused with his hand on the knob. "Jessica isn't like that. She has a head on her shoulders."

"Sometimes people lose their heads," Clyde told him, recalling Jessica's words to that effect.

Miles grinned. "Is that what happened to you two? You'll figure it out, bro," he said wisely and went inside. "Yo, Jessica, you here?"

Clyde, entering the house behind his brother, spotted Jessica by the steps. She was simply standing there, gazing out the front door window as if lost in thought. His heart roared up to mach speed.

"Hi, Miles," she said, turning and smiling as if delighted at their company. "I saw the truck leave a moment ago. I thought you would be right behind it."

"I'm giving it a head start," he said. "You're looking beautiful this morning. As usual."

"Thank you, kind sir." Her bright blue gaze flicked to Clyde, then back to Miles. "Have you had breakfast?"

"At dawn," he said. "I thought I'd grab a mug of coffee and head out."

Clyde glanced at the coffeemaker on the counter. A fresh pot of coffee was ready. Miles filled a plastic travel mug, gave Jessica a kiss on the cheek when she came into the kitchen, flicked a hard glance Clyde's way, then left.

The silence in the house hummed like a high-voltage wire after the door closed. In a couple of seconds they heard the sounds of a motor, then the crunch of tires on gravel as Miles headed after the cattle truck.

"Have you eaten?" Clyde asked.

"Not yet."

He was ravenous, he realized. But not for food. For her. For the taste and feel of her. "I skipped breakfast. I'll scramble some eggs for us."

"I'm not hungry." She didn't look at him. "There's really no reason I can't visit with my folks now. Roy hasn't found me, so he's probably gone on to someone else. It should be safe to leave."

Her laughter was soft, fluttery. It made him ache inside in ways he couldn't describe. That was the trouble with women, he decided. They got a man in knots, then they took off for parts unknown.

"Violet will be here for the wedding. You'll have to stay until after that."

Her eyes flicked to him. "Did she call?"

"Not recently. But she won't miss Steven's wedding. I assume she'll stay here. She likes the guesthouse. It's quieter than the Double Crown Ranch."

Jessica nodded. "She says there're too many people and too many things going on to really rest there."

"Right." He removed eggs, butter and milk from the fridge and prepared the meal, making enough for both of them. When the eggs and toast were ready, he divided the food between two plates and carried them to the dining table. "Bring us some milk," he said in casual tones.

She brought in two glasses of milk, then sat at her usual place to his right.

"Miles was right. You're quiet this morning." He inhaled deeply, released it. "I'm sorry about last night. I was taken by surprise. The situation raised old issues in my mind, and

I reacted without thinking. Miles says you're a square dealer. I think that, too."

Jessica was taken aback. She hadn't expected the apology. In fact, she'd thought he would be relieved to deliver her to her parents.

"I think you should stay here until we know where we stand," he continued.

"Until we know if I'm pregnant."

He nodded. "We can work it out from there. We can drive up to San Antonio on Monday and get a license. Just in case," he added in practical tones.

She knew the offer was due to his caring nature, which he tried to keep hidden, and she felt herself going all soft and feminine inside. She steeled herself against him. She didn't want duty. She wanted bliss and happiness and love.

"We'll wait," she said firmly. "As someone once said— don't count your chickens before they're hatched. We're not even sure we're incubating yet."

He shot her a somewhat irritated glance. "You don't seem worried about it."

"I'm lucky. I have enough money to make it on my own. A lot of women don't. They stay in a bad situation because they don't have the financial resources to get out."

He touched Jessica's cheek, liking the smoothness of her skin and the warmth of her. "Would it be such a terrible situation? I thought we worked well together…in many ways." He grinned as she shook her head.

"Men," she said, but with wry amusement in the smile that teased her lips. Rising, she carried her dishes to the kitchen and put them in the dishwasher.

Clyde relaxed and sipped the coffee, which was better than his usual brew. He realized he did feel sort of…well, noble and all that.

* * *

At eight that evening, Clyde was still in the office, trying to catch up on paperwork. He had to verify to the state that the egg operation was in compliance with environmental laws on manure disposal.

No problem there. When they'd started the business, Steven had researched the latest sewage treatment system. After the waste was processed, it was bagged and sold as organic fertilizer to a local home and garden store.

As he checked off each item on his to-do list, he kept an ear tuned to Jessica's movements in the house.

Earlier she'd been in the kitchen for a glass of water, which she'd taken upstairs. At present she was in her room, presumably reading the John Adams biography, no doubt tired from the afternoon she'd spent working on an old table she'd found in the storage shed. He wondered if she would come to him when it was time for bed.

Probably not.

There was no use torturing himself by dwelling on the possibility. They were at an impasse until they knew what the future held.

He sucked in a deep breath. A baby. A little boy or girl who would follow him around the ranch, full of wonder and questions about nature.

His mother would be in heaven. She was quite upset that her youngest child was in her thirties, Jack was forty, and not one of the five had produced grandkids. Her hopes were centered on Steven and Amy at present. Wouldn't it be a kick if he and Jessica had the first child?

Don't count your chickens….

Jessica was right. They would have to take it one day at a time until they knew what was what. He noted she'd avoided him since the conversation that morning although he'd stayed close to the house during the afternoon.

When he'd come in shortly before six, he'd found a casserole in the oven. A note on the fridge said a salad was inside and that she'd already eaten, so he was to help himself. Hearing water running in her quarters when he went up to wash and change clothes, he'd assumed she was taking a shower. He summoned all his self-control to subdue the urge to see if she would welcome him if he joined her.

He finished inputting data on the stock sale in the computer, saved, made a backup copy and turned the machine off. Glancing at the clock, he saw it was now after nine.

The phone rang.

"Flying Aces," he said.

"Hi, it's your favorite sister," Violet told him. "How are things going at the ranch?"

"Fine. Where are you?"

"I'm not sure. Somewhere on the ocean. They don't put up many signs out here."

He chuckled, then asked, "When will you be home? You will get in for Steven's wedding, won't you?"

"Yes. I spoke to Mom, so I know it's Friday. I'll arrive in port Wednesday and fly in to San Antonio that evening. Can you and Jessica pick me up?"

"Sure." He grabbed a pencil. "Okay, what's your flight number and time of arrival?"

After he wrote down the information, she asked, "Is Jessica available? I want to find out what she's wearing."

"Hold on." He went to the stairs and called up, "Jessica? It's Violet. She wants to talk to you."

"Okay. Thank you."

After he made sure the women were connected, he hung up the office phone. He'd noticed the perfect politeness in Jessica's voice when she'd taken the call. It was that of strangers, the way she'd been when she'd first arrived.

He paced restlessly through the house, not liking the distance she'd put between them. He liked being with her up close and personal, as one might say.

Hearing footsteps on the stairs, he turned from staring out the back door, where he'd ended up, and observed his guest as she descended and came down the hall.

She gestured toward the kitchen. "I thought I would have a snack."

He nodded and followed her into the other room. She made a cup of herbal tea and selected a banana to go with it. She added milk to the tea.

"You're eating more," he said.

"Yes. Smoky and I walk a lot, so I can indulge in a treat occasionally."

"I see."

He couldn't think of anything else to say. No idle chitchat came to mind. He wished he had Miles's gift for light conversation. It wasn't something he'd ever thought necessary to cultivate, but now he wished he had.

"Jessica—" he began, not at all sure what he was going to say.

"I'm going to bed," she said abruptly. Leaving the banana and taking the tea with her, she left the room.

He locked the doors before going upstairs. At her door, he paused. Hearing no sound, he continued to his own room.

He wanted to go to her and share all the wonder of that passion they experienced together.

Was there more?

Yes, he admitted. There was an intimacy greater than any he'd ever shared with anyone, excitement when he headed for the house, knowing she would be here, regret over maybe hurting her feelings…and a confused jumble of emotion during it all.

He sighed, feeling even more confused. Grabbing a book—he didn't even look at the title—he settled in the easy chair and began reading until he was ready to go to bed.

Eleven

"What do you think?" Jessica asked, standing back and looking the lyre table over.

"It's lovely," Cimma Perez assured her.

Jessica viewed the piece of furniture with a critical eye. She'd worked on it all Saturday afternoon. Today she'd given it a final polishing with paste wax. It now gleamed with the fine patina of age and TLC.

After hauling it out of the shed yesterday, she'd cleaned it and found the original finish in good shape. A light sanding had been all it needed before she'd used a wood sealer on it and glued the marble top back together.

She'd let the sealer and the glue dry overnight and now, after the waxing and lots of rubbing, the piece was perfect, with enough dings and nicks to indicate its long and useful life but not impair its beauty. The thin fracture line in the clean marble blended naturally with the other markings of the stone.

"I hope I age as well as this table has," she murmured.

Cimma thought this was funny. "You will be beautiful when you are very old."

Now it was Jessica's turn to grin. "I'll keep my fingers crossed. Thanks for your help."

She and Cimma had worked together on the polishing after the Perez family had returned from church that morning. Jessica had thought of joining her sister's family in Red Rock for services and perhaps lunch afterward, but Clyde had discouraged the idea.

Since he'd learned of the possibility of a child, he'd become much more concerned for her safety. She wasn't sure if this pleased or irritated her.

Glancing at her watch, she saw it was nearly four. "I'd better get ready. We're going to Steven's for dinner and a tour of his new place. That's why I wanted the table ready. I thought we could take it with us."

"What a thoughtful wedding gift," Cimma said, giving her a warm smile.

"I'd mentioned the piece to Amy and she'd seemed interested. I hope she likes it."

"She'll love it," the older woman predicted. "Well, I'd better head back to my place and make sure the kids have done their homework."

They said goodbye, then Jessica went inside and dashed up the stairs. Leaving her work clothes on the floor of the closet, she headed for the shower.

Twenty minutes later, she gazed at her clothing and tried to determine how casual the dinner was going to be. She finally decided blue slacks with a white silk blouse would fit any situation. She blow-dried her hair and dressed quickly upon hearing the shower come on next door.

With a light touch of makeup and her favorite pearl earrings, she was ready when she heard Clyde leave his room. She joined him in the gallery.

He, too, wore dark slacks and a white shirt, the cuffs rolled up on his strong sinewy forearms. His hair gleamed with healthy highlights, making her long to run her fingers through it.

His dark eyes flicked over her without expression, although a solemn smile appeared on his handsome face. "Very nice," he complimented.

"Thanks. Uh, would you help me put the table in the truck? Or were you going to use the station wagon?"

"It's already in the station wagon," he said.

"Oh. Good."

Awkward with him for reasons she couldn't define, she let him usher her to the vehicle. She was aware of the currents that flowed between them and the silence that filled the air with the electric hum of tension.

It seemed forever before they arrived at Steven's newly remodeled home on the legendary Loma Vista Ranch near the outskirts of Austin. The ranch had been established way back in the true Wild West days, if Jessica remembered correctly from conversations with Violet. It consisted of ten thousand acres of the finest rangeland in the state.

Another car was in the drive next to a landscaped path that led to a charming front door of oak and glass panels.

Steven must have been watching for them. He opened the door as soon as they appeared. "Come in. We're having a glass of wine on the patio." He gave Jessica a hug and extended a hand to his triplet.

"Who's here?" Clyde asked as they went through the house to the patio overlooking the rolling green acres dotted with cattle.

"Ryan and Peter Clark stopped by. They were playing golf over at Onion Creek. I think you've met Peter," Steven said to Clyde. "He's a neurosurgeon here in Austin and a friend of Ryan's family."

"Yes, I remember him."

The doors were open to the patio. Amy and the two men stood. Jessica received a warm hug from Amy, then one from Ryan, who refused to stand on formalities.

"I watched you grow up, young lady," he said, tapping her chin with his forefinger, then holding her arms wide as he looked her over affectionately. "The end result is quite lovely, I might add."

Jessica bobbed a curtsy and murmured her thanks. She shook hands with Peter Clark when Steven finished with the introductions. Peter was a handsome man with green eyes, dark hair and a firm handshake.

Soon they were all settled in cushioned patio chairs and served their choice in wine. Jessica chose a rosé while Clyde accepted a glass of deep red cabernet.

"Steven says you're a neurosurgeon?" she inquired of the doctor after the men had discussed the new ranch.

"Yes, in Austin."

"Then you probably know Violet," Jessica deduced since the two were in the same profession.

"Our sister," Clyde said, gesturing to himself and Steven.

"I recall the name, but we've never met," Peter said politely.

"She's a neurologist," Jessica told him. She turned to Steven and Amy. "Did Clyde tell you she called to say she'll be home in time for the wedding?"

Amy nodded. "She called and told us the news, too. I'm so glad the whole family will be here."

"Wait a minute," Peter said suddenly. "Is Violet the same Dr. Fortune who wrote a paper on aging diseases of the brain and has done extensive research in the field?"

"Yes, that's her." Jessica was pleased that he'd heard of her friend.

"It was a brilliant piece of work," Peter said in an admiring manner.

"I'll tell her you said that," Jessica promised.

"Violet and Jessica are the best of friends," Clyde explained to the doctor. "Be careful what you say to one because the other will hear of it immediately."

After the others laughed, Ryan asked, "Has there been a lot of progress on the malfunctions of the brain of late? I haven't read of anything new in a while."

"Stem cell research holds the most promise for long-term diseases," Peter said. "As a surgeon, I've been studying implanting techniques for new tissue, with the hope that the procedure will become available someday."

"But not for a long time," Ryan concluded.

"No, I'm afraid not. We know a lot about the brain, but it's only a scratch on the surface of the knowledge that is still to be discovered."

"Breakthroughs can happen at any time, according to Violet. She says great strides are being made throughout the world. I know she would love to talk to you about it," Jessica said sincerely to the neurosurgeon. "She's due in from her cruise on Wednesday."

"I'll look forward to meeting her," Peter said with a smile.

"So will I," Ryan murmured in a thoughtful manner. "It seems an age since she spent any time at the Double Crown. Maybe we can lure her there for a visit after the wedding."

Clyde stood. "That reminds me. I could use some help bringing in a special wedding present."

"You and Miles have already given us that magnificent bull," Amy said.

"This one's special for you. Stay here until I tell you to come," Clyde told her. "I'll need your strong back," he said to his brother.

The two men went to the station wagon while the other four stayed on the patio. In a minute they could hear the two brothers in the foyer of the elegant home. There was a hushed discussion, then Clyde called, "Okay. You can come out here now."

Amy led the way into the house. She stopped at the arch-way of the entrance hall. "Oh!" she said. "Oh, how lovely!" She walked all around the lyre table, which now held pride of place in the center of the marble floor. "This is perfect, absolutely perfect."

Jessica sighed in relief at the obvious pleasure on Amy's face.

"I know who to thank for it, too," the other woman continued, turning to Jessica. "When did you find the time to restore it?"

"It was actually in good shape. Clinton's wife helped me polish it so we could bring it over today."

"Thank you so much. I love it," Amy assured her.

Jessica found herself being warmly hugged again by both Amy and Steven. After everyone had properly admired the piece, Ryan and Peter said they needed to leave.

The others waved them off from the front door before returning to the patio. "Let's eat out here, shall we?" Steven asked his bride-to-be.

She nodded. "That would be lovely."

"Is there anything I can do?" Jessica asked.

Amy looked mischievous. "I must confess—we had a caterer deliver the meal. It's in the oven, so all we have to do is bring it out. But first, I thought you might enjoy a tour of the house."

"I would love it," Jessica said.

"Come on, bro. I want to show you *my* new office," Steven said to Clyde.

The men argued over who had the best equipment and latest ranching programs on their computers until Amy and Jessica rolled their eyes and burst out laughing.

"Let me show you my favorite thing." Amy led the way into the master suite and bath.

"This is the most gorgeous bathroom I've ever seen," Jessica said of the spa tub and separate steam shower, all done in the most luxurious of tiles. "It's even more impressive than those I saw at the Double Crown Ranch when I was a teenager."

Amy laughed in delight. "I do love our home. I want lots of family and friends to stay with us and feel comfortable here, the same as Steven and I do."

"How could one help it?" Jessica gestured around a large comfortable guest suite when they went to the next room. "The problem might be in getting them to leave."

After the grand tour, they went to the kitchen and prepared their plates, then settled on the patio as the soft glow of sunset segued into the enchanted shades of twilight.

Jessica realized how easy it would be to imagine that she and Clyde were a couple in love as Steven and Amy were, that they would always be together like this.

"So what's the plan on the big bash for Ryan?" Clyde asked while they dined on baked Cornish hens with pecan-herb stuffing and an assortment of vegetables.

Amy sighed while Steven looked amused. "We've settled on a date in November," she said. "After the election."

Steven patted her shoulder. "Don't look so worried. I'm sure the dear governor will be reelected. Even if he isn't, he's still the glorious leader until the end of the year and can give the state's humanitarian award to Ryan. Things are falling into place," he said with a loving glance at his fiancée.

"Planning two major events, one of them being your own wedding, would drive me right over the edge," Jessica declared, casting Amy an admiring glance.

"It has been difficult. So much seems to be happening lately, unfortunately, not all of it good," Amy said.

Clyde nodded. "Any further word on Christopher Jamison's murderer?"

"Not that I've heard." Steven refilled their wineglasses and resumed his seat. "Ryan is frustrated that there have been no breaks in the case."

After discussing the seemingly endless investigation, they turned to the wedding plans. The ceremony itself would be at a small church in Austin that Amy had attended most of her life. A quiet, intimate reception would be held here at the couple's home.

Jessica refused to feel envious as they talked of the coming nuptials, but later, on the way back to the Flying Aces homestead, she couldn't help but wish for a wonderful future for her and the silent man beside her. Sharing life—home, children, memories—established strong bonds between a man and woman. And love could grow from that.

The phone was ringing when Jessica went downstairs Monday morning. She ignored it while pouring a cup of coffee, but hesitated before sitting in her usual place at the island counter. She heard Steven's voice on the answering machine telling whoever it was to leave a message. When she heard her sister's voice, she dashed for the portable kitchen phone.

"Leslie? Don't hang up. It's me," she said. "Hold on while I turn off the machine."

The beep indicated the caller could begin a message. She ran into the office and turned off the machine. "Hi," she said when that was done. She returned to the stool in the kitchen. "What's happening with you?"

"The usual," Leslie said. "I'm going into San Antonio today to look at some bridal items for the store. Would you be available?"

"Yes!"

Leslie laughed at her enthusiasm. "Going a little stir-crazy, are we?"

"Not at all, but it would be wonderful to see you. Also I might shop for a wedding outfit—"

"What?"

"For Steven and Amy's wedding on Friday," she explained. "I only brought my hiding-out wardrobe with me. I didn't think I would need glamorous stuff, too."

"You always look great," Leslie complained albeit good-naturedly. "I'm the one who should shop. I've lost fifteen pounds."

"Wow. Let me buy you something extravagant to celebrate," Jessica proposed. "Something to remind Marty just why he married you."

"Well," Leslie murmured drolly, "I was preggie, and our parents were angry. I'm not sure I want to remind him of those good ol' days."

"Oops, I'd forgotten. There was a big, ahem, discussion of the issues in our family living room."

They laughed together. In addition to familial love for her sister, Jessica felt the deep affection that came from shared experiences, and knew it was returned. She was still smiling when Clyde came inside. He went to the kitchen sink and got a glass of water, which he drank down without pause.

"Right," Leslie said. "You stood up for us and insisted

that we make up our own minds about what we wanted to do. You even agreed to pay for tuition and babysitting if I wanted to go to college. I've never forgotten how generous you were."

"I had a lot of money by then," Jessica reminded her sister airily. "I liked throwing it around to show what a big wheel I was."

Leslie cracked up at this claim. "Yeah, right."

Clyde turned and leaned against the counter, one eyebrow going up in a quizzical fashion at her statement.

"Hold on," Jessica said into the phone. To Clyde she said, "This is Leslie. We're heading for the city today. I want to get an outfit for the wedding."

"What about the marriage license?" he asked.

She gaped at him in surprise. "I thought we'd agreed to wait until we knew...until later," she finished lamely.

"Is that Clyde?" Leslie demanded in her ear. "Did he say marriage license? For you two? What's going on?"

"Nothing," Jessica said into the phone. "Hold on." She laid her palm over the receiver. "Could we discuss this later?" she requested.

He shrugged, but his stare was dark and rather moody, as if displeased about the whole situation. She hadn't agreed to actually get the license. Had she? She tried to recall their conversations on the subject, but Leslie was yammering excitedly about wedding plans for them.

"Leslie," she said firmly into the phone. "Clyde and I are not getting married."

"But you have discussed the possibility, haven't you?"

It wasn't really a question. Her sister had already leaped to a hundred conclusions about them, ninety-nine of them wrong.

Another idea came to Leslie. "Ohmigosh, Jess, are you pregnant?"

It was, of course, the one thing she was right about.

"I'll talk to you later," Jessica promised while a storm cloud settled in Clyde's eyes.

"I'll pick you up in a hour, okay?" her sister said. "I expect a full accounting of recent events."

"Yes, yes, that's fine. I'll see you then." She hit the off button and picked up her coffee cup. She hid behind the steamy vapor rising from it as she sipped and waited for the inquisition from her host.

Clyde glanced at the microwave clock. "I need a part for the tractor. If I go to the dealer's place and pick it up this morning, I can meet you and your sister in San Antonio for lunch around one."

"That would be nice," she said, doubt in every word.

His eyebrow rose slightly, mirroring his skeptical attitude. "Then we can get the marriage license."

"I thought we'd agreed to take it one day at a time until we know for sure what the future holds."

His broad chest rose and fell in an exasperated breath. "I like things settled. Besides, we have to think of the child."

As if that wasn't the first thing she thought of each morning and the last thing at night! Well, maybe there were a couple of other things that occurred to her at night.

His scowl grew more pronounced. "What's so funny?"

"Us."

She held her smile, inviting him to see the humor in the situation. Finally he shook his head while a grin reluctantly bloomed on his handsome face. "Babies complicate things."

"I didn't realize how much," she admitted. "I thought sex was supposed to be simple in this day and age, sort of 'and a good time was had by all' event. This puts a whole new spin on it, doesn't it?"

"Yeah." He brushed his fingers through his hair, then rubbed the back of his neck. "Funny, but having a kid appeals to me. I've never thought much about it. That was Jack's department. Steven, Miles and I were the diehard bachelors."

"Well, I've certainly learned my lesson," she continued wryly. "Use proper caution in all things."

"No more losing your head at the lake, huh?" he murmured, surprising her with the teasing tone.

"Absolutely not." She checked the time. "I'd better eat, then get ready. Leslie will be here soon." She paused. "Are you really going to meet us at lunch?"

He waved the idea aside. "I'll let you girls have your fun. Just how much are you going to tell your sister about what happened between us?"

"I think I'll have to tell all, or else she'll hound me to death about the marriage license."

"Should I be ready for a visit from your outraged parents?"

She smiled and shook her head. "She won't tell. Sisters always stick together."

"Just like brothers. We always covered for each other with the parents."

"With three of you, it would be a natural thing to do." Her eyes opened wide. "Clyde," she said in a shaken voice, "what do we do if…we have triplets?"

He, too, was obviously startled by the thought. "Call in reinforcements, I suppose."

They stared at each other for a long second, then burst into laughter, as if it were the funniest thing either had ever heard.

Twilight had fallen by the time Leslie and Jessica neared the ranch. They had made a full day of the shopping trip to San Antonio, lingering for two hours over lunch and catching up on all the little details of each other's lives.

They'd shopped at large department stores and tiny boutiques until they'd found just the right outfits.

Glancing behind them, Jessica noted the vehicle that had stayed an even distance behind them for several miles. She wondered if it was Clyde, coming back from his trip to get the tractor part. A smile sprang to her lips.

Tired but happy, she breathed deeply and let her mind drift as her sister turned onto the ranch driveway, then stopped close to the house.

"I hate for the day to end," Leslie said.

"Me, too." Jessica climbed out and gathered her packages—the dress and a pair of pumps—before leaning back inside the car and giving Leslie a buss on the cheek. "I can't remember when I've had such a lovely day."

"Same here."

After Leslie swung the car around and headed back down the drive, Jessica noticed the other car had gone by the ranch drive and was heading on down the road. Not Clyde, then. She wondered where he was. The house was dark.

Her good feelings diminished a bit as she entered the back door and flicked on the lights in the kitchen. Seeing a note on the refrigerator, she read it and discovered her host had gone to Austin to try and find the part he needed.

Knowing why he wasn't at the house made her feel much better. Frowning at herself for reacting to his absence, she went upstairs, hung her new dress in the closet, then slipped into her gown and robe. She still had that thick biography to finish.

And only three days left to do it, she realized. Thursday, after the wedding, she would move to her parents' home in Austin. She'd called and they were expecting her.

Halfway across the room, she stopped abruptly and stared at the bed. Her heart stopped, then raced like an Indy

500 car. "Oh-h-h," she murmured as an irrepressible smile spread over her face.

On her pillow lay one perfect rose, deep pink and exquisitely beautiful.

She sank down on the side of the bed and lifted the flower, holding it between her breasts as she inhaled its delicate scent. It was from a bush growing beside the walkway in front of the house. All the thorns had been removed along the stem.

That was so like Clyde, she mused, closing her eyes, which suddenly stung with tears as a welter of emotions ran through her. He was a protective man, and a caring one. He would be a wonderful husband and father.

Inhaling the delicate fragrance of the rose, she thought of their laughter that morning when they'd realized they could have triplets. That moment and the shared laughter had signaled a change between them. For that instant, they'd shared a sweet closeness as they'd realized exactly what fate could have in store for them.

More than anything she'd ever wanted, she realized she wanted him in her life, in her arms, her heart. Perhaps it was time to tell him that very thing. Her heart singing, she put the rose in a glass of water and prepared to wait up for his return, no matter how late that was.

Twelve

Arriving home shortly after dark that night, Clyde frowned upon spotting the open pasture gate. It wasn't like his brother to forget something as important as a gate.

Hmm, Miles had taken the RV and moved to the northern sector of the ranch to join the ranch hands in combing the gullies and ravines of the rough country for cattle. The gate hadn't been open at that time. They would have noticed it. That left Jessica.

He tried to excuse her carelessness due to lack of knowledge, but she was a local girl. She knew the value of stock and the importance of secure fences and gates.

If she didn't do it, that left rustlers as the likely culprits. He would have to check it out.

A perfect ending to a perfect day. It had started out on a wrong note and gotten worse from there. He'd had to chase all over the state to find a replacement part for the tractor. Now he'd have to chase all over the county if the cattle had gotten out.

Or call the sheriff if they'd been stolen. He sighed. That would make for a long night.

He glanced at the house as he stepped down from the truck and headed for the gate. Lights were on downstairs, and another gleamed from Jessica's room. He wondered if she was still awake. It wasn't all that late—a bit after ten.

As usual, everything in his body came alive at the thought of her. He smiled as he thought of her shock at the idea of triplets. It was possible, he supposed.

He grabbed the gate and swung it shut with a clang, hearing the latch snap securely into place.

At that moment, another sound caught his attention. He turned his head and heard an odd *thud* that seemed to echo through his skull. An explosion of pain followed, then the night closed around him, smothering the last desperate thought in his mind.

Jessica.

Jessica listened, but didn't hear anything. She laid the book aside, pulled on her soft slippers and went downstairs to check for Clyde. It was long past time for him to return. She glanced at the clock on the stove. After ten.

Not that she was worried. Clyde could certainly take care of himself.

After making a cup of tea, she paced restlessly to the window and peered into the night. Ah, the pickup truck was visible as a silhouette against the outside light mounted on a tall pole beside the barn.

Her heart went into a nosedive.

Giving herself a good scolding for being concerned about his late arrival, she picked up the teacup and headed for the stairs. She didn't want to be caught hovering at the door like an anxious wife.

Her frown softened when her gaze fell on the lovely rose she'd placed on the bedside table. An idea came to her.

Without giving herself time for second thoughts, she propped herself on the pillows, arranged her nightgown in demure folds down to her ankles and then, smiling wickedly, she tucked the rose into the gown so that it nestled in the valley between her breasts. She smoothed her hair so that it lay in a shining mass over each shoulder.

Excitement pounded a heady refrain in time with her heart when she felt a draft of air swirl into the room. She hadn't heard the back door open and close, but she knew Clyde had entered the house.

Because there might be a child and because he was the one who'd mentioned marriage, she thought it was time they had a serious talk, not only about the future, but about what they honestly felt for each other.

Hearing a creak of wood from the steps, she took a deep breath and called, "Clyde?"

Nothing but silence replied for long moments.

She listened intently for his approach to her door, but it never came.

Nothing.

Without quite knowing how she knew, she was positive he was standing just outside her door. She opened her mouth to call his name again, then stopped.

A chill, like cold, bony fingers, stroked her neck. Whoever was out there wasn't Clyde. She knew it instinctively. She rose and pulled on her slippers and the blue robe. Her heart beat fast, but this time it was from some deeply ingrained fear for survival.

She crossed the room and slipped silently into the closet. Crouching behind the all-purpose raincoat, she placed her suitcase so that it blocked her lower legs from view. Then she waited.

A whisper of sound warned her that someone was in the bedroom. She forced her breath into a quiet rhythm of calm.

She heard a soft click. Light appeared under the closet door. The prowler had flicked on the bathroom light.

The silence was followed by two quick steps, then the closet door was wrenched open and thrown back on its hinges so hard it hit the doorstop with a loud bang.

She flinched but made no noise.

A moment stretched into an eternity, then the fear eased. She realized he'd left. Ever so slowly, she leaned past the raincoat sleeve and peered out.

The closet door had been left open. She could see most of the bedroom. No one was there.

A sound from the gallery told her the intruder was heading toward Clyde's bedroom. She eased out of her hiding place, tiptoed to the door, then cautiously peered out. She saw nothing.

Not wasting a second, she ran silently down the steps, careful of the one that sometimes squeaked. She made it to the bottom step. There, she stepped on a hammer—where had that come from?—tripped and fell to her hands and knees on the floor. In a flash she was up and running for the door.

Hoping to delay the prowler, she flicked out the lights she'd left on inside the house for Clyde and yanked open the door. Footsteps running along the gallery warned her that she didn't have much time. She headed for the creek.

For once she was grateful for darkness. The waning moon was only a sliver in the night sky. Ducking behind a tall photinia shrub, she kept it between her and the house as she sprinted for the trees along the noisy stream.

Something cold touched her hand. She jerked and stifled a scream. "Smoky," she said, her heart in her throat.

The dog ran ahead of her, stopped, then leaped at the flying hem of her robe as she passed him.

"No," she said on a gasp.

He dropped his tail at the reprimand and loped along beside her, apparently thinking they were having a jog as they often did during the afternoon.

Upon reaching the trees, Jessica stopped and leaned a hand against the rough bark of one while she looked behind and checked on the whereabouts of the prowler.

The stalker, she corrected.

The same instincts that had told her to run also identified the man in the house as Roy Balter, the one who had haunted her in New York until she'd run away.

She pressed a hand to her breast. The rose was gone. It must have fallen while she ran. Useless tears misted her vision for a second. How stupid of her to think Clyde had given her the eternal symbol of love.

Blinking, she spotted a shadow moving from the photinia bush to the path she'd followed to the creek. He moved swiftly but with surefooted ease in an easy lope that ate up the distance. She headed straight into the creek.

The water rose to her knees, then to midthigh. She held her gown and robe up as best she could. A gasp escaped her when she slid on a slick rock and hit her knee on another. Pushing upright from a larger boulder, she held on to it while she found her footing, then made it out of the water and to shore once more.

Behind her, she heard Smoky whine as he ran along the edge of the creek, then a splash as he leaped in so he could follow her.

She didn't wait, but ran as fast as she ever had up the hill that obscured the egg barn and beyond that, Clinton's house. She would find refuge there.

Halfway up the hill, Smoky caught up and raced along beside her, no longer thinking this was a game. He seemed to know the pack was in trouble and kept glancing behind them.

When Jessica looked back, she saw the dark shadow of the man coming up the hill at an incredible pace. He wore all black and only his face and hands gleamed in the inky darkness like those of a dismembered ghost.

Fear gave her an adrenaline boost, but she couldn't keep ahead. As she neared the top of the hill, she heard his steps right behind her. With one more burst of speed, she broached the hillock.

That was as far as she got.

Her wrist was caught in an iron clasp. He wrenched her arm upward in a sharp angle and pressed it against her back. She fell on her face into the grass.

Beside her, Smoky whimpered near her ear and leaped around in nervous excitement.

"Got you," Roy said, his voice low but triumphant.

She tried to push upright, but his knee settled in the center of her back, trapping her hand under it so she couldn't move her right arm. His weight increased, slowly pressing the air from her lungs.

"Leave me alone," she said fiercely. "I haven't done anything to you. Leave me alone."

He gathered her hair into one hand and pulled, lifting her head at a painful tilt. Leaning down, he smiled into her face like a feral animal finally catching its prey.

"You're mine," he whispered. "You ran away. Now you must be punished."

He stroked along her throat with something cold and thin. She realized he had a knife.

For a split second she thought of Clyde and their child and a future that would never be.

Closing out the despair, she sought calm. "What do you

want?" she asked, hoping to buy time to find a way out of this nightmare.

He laughed. "Heh, heh-heh."

Her skin crawled at the familiar sound. Hatred flooded through her, a riptide of anger, fear and outrage that he should do this to her.

"Get off me!" Ignoring pain in her arm and scalp, she thrust herself to the side. New pain lanced through her shoulder, but she managed to unseat him, then kick him, her heel landing with a solid thud on his chin.

"Bitch," he snarled.

She rolled away, helped by the downward slope of the hill. "Get him, Smoky! Get him!"

Leaping to her feet, she surprised her attacker by charging into him at high speed and again caught him on the chin, this time with the full force of her raised knee.

Smoky, barking excitedly, leaped on, too.

"Damn dog," Roy said, then cursed as Smoky sunk his teeth into the man's forearm and held on.

Jessica skirted the struggling pair and headed for the Perez home. Its windows were dark, but she was sure they were home since this was a weekday and the kids had school the next day. She ran like the wind, as if a thousand demons were on her heels.

Behind her, she heard sudden, sharp yelps of pain from Smoky and remembered the cold steel of the knife at her throat. Sorrow joined all the other emotions that throbbed in her. She was sure Roy had stabbed the dog. The harsh cries of the injured animal continued as she set her sights and all her remaining energy on reaching the house.

"Clinton!" she screamed when she was near enough that they might hear. "Cimma! Help! Help!"

A light came on inside. Then another. And another. Everyone was awake.

The front door opened just as she stumbled over the porch. She fell inside and into Clinton's arms.

"Call the police," she said, gasping for breath and holding her aching side. "A man...the stalker..."

"It's all right," Clinton said. "Cimma's on the phone with the sheriff now. Nothing's going to hurt you."

Holding his arm, she pushed herself upright. That was when she noticed both the teenage son and daughter held rifles in their hands. Their serious young faces indicated they were ready to use them.

"Thank goodness," she said and, to her shame, began to weep.

Clyde fought wave after wave of nausea and pain. There was one thought in his mind. Find Jessica.

He didn't know who attacked him, whether it was something as simple as a rustler or if it was her stalker, but he knew in his bones that she was in danger.

Pushing himself to his knees, he held on to the fence and got to his feet. The lights went off in the house at the instant he turned in that direction.

A ghostly shape ran across the patio and disappeared on the path to the creek. Shortly after that, another figure ran in the same direction.

His brain reeling like that of a drunk, he lunged after the fleeing twosome. The pain in his head was no worse than that in his heart. He'd failed to keep his word. He'd failed to protect Jessica from the madman who was hunting her. He'd even wondered for a time if there was a madman.

"Dear God," he murmured.

That was all he could get out, but it was a prayer for her safety, that he could get to her in time.

Thought disappeared as seconds stretched into agonizing moments. His head pounded with each footfall, so hard it felt as if an artery would burst if he didn't stop.

He kept on, knowing a grimness of spirit like none other he'd ever experienced.

Jessica. Jessica.

Her name echoed inside him with each step he took.

Save her. Must save her, some fierce unforgiving part of him repeated over and over.

He heard her scream for help when he reached the creek. He stumbled into the water, fell, rose and pushed on in a half crouch, using both hands to steady himself across the slippery rocks.

As he cleared the line of trees on the other side, he heard a sound that turned his blood cold—the horrible yelp of an animal injured beyond bearing.

"Bastard," he muttered and rushed up the hill at a desperate run. Pain disappeared. A red haze shrouded his mind so that he felt nothing now but a rage so deep it reached his soul.

When he topped the hill, he found only one person. Roy Balter drew his hand back again, ready to plunge the knife into the dog once more.

Clyde leaped at the stalker in a flying tackle he hadn't tried since he'd played college football. He and the villain met in a deadly tangle of arms and legs and the slashing blade.

Clyde rolled on top. He smashed Roy in the mouth. "For Jessica," he said. He hit him again. "For Smoky." A third time. "For all the others you've frightened and hurt."

Clyde stopped and waited, but Balter didn't move. His hand opened and the knife dropped from his grasp. Clyde grabbed it and stuck it in the waistband of his jeans.

Removing a handkerchief from his pocket, he tied the stalker's hands behind his back, then yanked him to his feet when he opened his eyes.

Clyde noted there were lights on at Clinton's house. Jessica had made it there, he hoped. Using the knife tip, he prodded Balter into heading that way, then scooped Smoky into his arms, keeping the knife ready just in case his prisoner tried anything. Part of him wished he would.

Blood lust, once aroused, was slow to fade, he found.

Just before they reached the porch, sirens and flashing lights appeared from two directions on the highway. Help was on its way. He became aware of the pounding in his head and pressed a hand to the back. He recognized the warm ooze of blood from his scalp.

"Clinton!" he called at the door.

When Clinton and his son came out, Clyde smiled at them. "Got a skunk for you," he said, pushing Balter forward. "Smoky needs some help."

The world swirled dangerously. There was one more thing he had to know. "Did Jessica make it here?"

"Yes," Clinton said in an oddly choked voice. "Son, take the dog. Here, lean on me. Give me the knife."

Clyde laid an arm over Clinton's shoulders, handed over the bloody blade and passed right out.

Jessica woke as light streamed into the room. For a second, she didn't know where she was. A glance reminded her she was in Clyde's hospital room in San Antonio.

He still slept, but it was a peaceful sleep now. He'd been restless until she'd been allowed to see him. He'd held her hand, gazed at her in a solemn way, then had quit fighting the injury and fatigue and gone to sleep.

She, too, had slept, settling in the recliner in his room with a pillow and blanket. She'd rested calmly, knowing the man she hated was behind bars and the one she loved was safe and okay…well, nearly okay. He would need a few days of rest due to the concussion.

She clenched her teeth in a silent snarl. Roy had opened the pasture gate, then waited for Clyde. He'd sneaked up behind and hit the rancher with a hammer when Clyde closed the gate. She mentally called the villain all the names her parents had forbidden her to use.

A slight groan escaped her when she tried to stretch. With cautious fingers she examined the bandage on her shoulder. The knife had gone deep enough to slice into the muscle, but not so bad that she'd needed to be hospitalized.

Internal stitches had repaired the muscle while staples— she had to grin at the idea of being held together with staples—secured the flesh wound.

"What time is it?" Clyde asked, his voice raspy.

"Nearly seven." She rose and went to the side of his bed. "Breakfast will be served soon. Are you hungry?"

"I don't know. Where am I?"

She told him. "You have a concussion and a hairline fracture in your skull."

"Balter hit me," he concluded.

"Yes. Luckily you were wearing a hat. The doctors concluded the blow landed on the leather band, which absorbed a lot of the force."

Dark eyes searched over her whole body then returned to her face. "Are you all right?"

"Pretty much. I have a cut on the shoulder, but it wasn't serious." She smiled at him. "It was rather bloody, though. Scared the heck out of Clinton and his family when I stumbled into the house. When you arrived with a prisoner, looking even worse and wielding a bloody knife, they were speechless."

"Smoky—"

"—is fine," she quickly assured him. "Clinton said the vet patched him up, gave him an IV and antibiotics and declared him 'a survivor.'" Her voice faltered. "He saved my life," she said in a hoarse whisper. "He distracted Roy long enough for me to get away."

A cold, fierce anger flicked through Clyde's narrowed gaze, reminding her of ancient warrior kings.

"I knew he was a good dog," he said in a husky tone after a strained moment. His chest rose and fell in a deep breath. "How long do I have to stay here?"

"Until this afternoon. It's for observation. The nurse said it was standard procedure for concussions."

He nodded. "Is there any coffee?"

"I'll get it." She smiled and left the room.

During the day, a steady stream of visitors came by to check on the injured twosome. When Miles said the incident had made national news that morning, Clyde called his parents to assure them he and Jessica were fine. He told them as much as he remembered, then let Jessica tell her side of the story.

"There was a lovely rose on my pillow," she told them, indignant about that fact. "I thought—" She stopped upon realizing she couldn't voice exactly what she'd thought. "I should have known he'd left it," she continued. She told them of the roses left in her New York condo and how that had been the final straw that had driven her from the city to rural Texas.

When she hung up, both Clyde and Miles were staring at her in a way that made her uncomfortable. "What?" she asked.

"You didn't tell us about the roses," Miles scolded. "You didn't tell us about the petals being cut in half. That definitely indicated a psychotic mind."

"Just who did you think the rose was from?" Clyde demanded, then winced as pain lanced through his head.

Jessica's expression closed as if a veil had been drawn

across her features. "I really couldn't imagine," she said in a bland tone.

He knew she was lying. He also knew he had to learn the truth. It was vitally important.

"Well," Miles said casually, "I'd better get back to the ranch and, uh, take care of things there. Jessica, you have the keys to the station wagon?"

"Yes. Thanks for arranging to bring it here. The doctor said there was no reason I couldn't drive us home this afternoon if Clyde had no problems from the concussion."

"He has a hard head," Miles stated, giving his brother a sardonic glance. "A very hard head. Dense, in fact."

"I think we get the idea," Clyde said, threatening his triplet with a narrowed glance. He really wanted to be alone with Jessica.

Laughing, Miles left, only to be replaced by Steven and Amy. They were followed by Jessica's sister and mother.

More visitors came after lunch. Clyde relaxed and let Jessica retell the story to each group. With each telling, he relived the fear that drove him up the hill toward the struggling couple. The protective anger rose, making his head pound. He forced himself to stop thinking about it.

However, when they were alone and free of interruption, he had several questions that needed answers. He never got to ask them.

"Hello, is this the room of the great hero, Clyde Fortune?" a feminine voice inquired sweetly.

"Violet!" Jessica said, shock on her face. "How did you get here? You're supposed to be on a ship somewhere."

"One can leave the ship via helicopter," Violet explained, "and a credit card with a high limit."

His sister gave each of them a careful hug. Although her manner was bright and teasing, he could detect worry in the depths of her eyes, which were light blue like Jessica's.

He didn't recall noticing that fact in the past. But then, he hadn't been involved with his sister's best friend, either. He listened as Jessica went over the story yet again. They discussed the adventure the way women usually did, with both talking at once, backtracking to add salient details, asking questions and becoming incredulous or indignant or whatever the moment called for.

It made him smile just to listen to them.

Violet informed them she would act as their driver on the trip back to the ranch. She'd already cleared it with the doctor, who would dismiss him around two that afternoon.

Shortly before that time, Ryan Fortune appeared. He looked each of the patients over in his usual affectionate way. Both Clyde and Jessica assured him that they had suffered no long-lasting injuries.

"I'm relieved to hear it. Have you called your parents to tell them?" he asked them both.

Once they assured him of that, they chatted about Balter and the mind-set of a stalker and why he acted as he did.

"Death is the ultimate possession," Ryan told them. He pressed his fingers to one temple as if the thought gave him pain, then he smiled at Violet and asked, "Did you enjoy your cruise?"

"Very much." She told them amusing stories of the voyage and of the souvenirs she'd bought. "I'm going to look very exotic in a sarong and seashell earrings. I thought I might wear the outfit to Steven's wedding, but I'm not sure about shoes. The islanders were all barefoot."

That brought a laugh and several suggestions for proper footwear for the wedding. They deemed that flowers stuck between her toes would be highly appropriate.

"I'll think about it," she told them.

"When do you return to New York?" Ryan asked.

A quietness entered her expression. "I'm not sure. I've taken an extended leave to…think about things."

"Hmm," the Fortune patriarch said. He checked his watch. "It's time for me to go. Will you walk me out?" he asked Violet.

"Of course."

Violet waited while Ryan said his farewells to her brother and friend, then she fell into step with him as they walked down the corridor of the busy hospital.

"I have some questions to ask," he said in a low voice. "There's a garden through here that's usually quiet. Let's go there and talk."

She nodded and went with him to a bench under a shady arbor. After they sat down, Ryan was silent for a minute.

"This is a professional question," he began. "I don't want to alarm Lily or the rest of the family."

She nodded again. Most men didn't want their wives to know they were ill, especially if it might be serious. The women, sensing something was wrong, worried anyway.

"I'm having headaches," he said.

"Severe?" she asked, at once checking him for symptoms.

He hesitated. "Yes, I'm afraid so. They're becoming more frequent and getting worse. Is there any way you could check it out without, uh, a lot of fuss?"

"Without your family knowing," she concluded.

"There's no need to worry them."

"I'd be glad to do it," she assured him. "When would be a good time?"

"I thought perhaps after the wedding. You could come out to the Double Crown to visit for a few days."

She mentally consulted the events of the week. "After the wedding I want to stay with Clyde and Jessica for a couple of days. They'll need some TLC while they heal.

How about early next week? I could come over on Monday and stay a few days."

"That would be great. I appreciate it."

Her sense of responsibility as a physician made her ask, "Is the pain general or localized on one side?"

He rubbed one temple. "Mostly on this side, but not always."

"I see. Can you follow my finger with just your eyes? Don't rotate your head." She raised a finger and slowly moved it to the far right side, then to the far left.

After a couple of simple tests, she said they could do a more extensive medical workup the following week. "Then we can decide where to go from there."

He thanked her and left to return to his home, while Violet returned to Clyde's room. The doctor was there when she arrived. "Take them home," he told her. "They're both as tough as nails."

Thirty minutes later, on the way to the Flying Aces, Violet informed them she would be on hand to take care of them until Monday, then she was going to Ryan's home to visit for a few days.

"I wondered what he wanted to talk to you about," Jessica murmured from the backseat.

Jessica had good instincts about people, and Violet realized it was going to be hard to keep secrets from her best friend if Ryan was indeed ill.

Headaches could indicate a lot of things, some serious, some not so serious. Until she did a complete physical checkup, she wouldn't know if the elder and much-loved family patriarch had a problem.

Glancing at her brother, sitting silently in the passenger seat, she was grateful his injury wasn't worse.

Maybe, she thought wryly, the hammer blow had knocked some sense into him. He was quieter than ever, she noticed on the trip home, as if lost in deep, dark thoughts.

At any rate, a good doctor knew when to keep her mouth shut, particularly when she couldn't decide on her own future. The haunting sadness of late settled on her shoulders like an unwelcome blanket.

Meeting Jessica's eyes in the rearview mirror, she managed a smile. Her friend returned it, but her mood was obviously solemn as she gazed out the side window and watched the countryside flow past.

Thirteen

Clyde waited, as patient as a saint, for dinner to be served and done with. He and Jessica sat in lounge chairs under the patio arbor while Violet and Miles prepared the food on the grill. Steven and Amy brought plates, silverware and napkins from the house and set the table. All were determined to lavish TLC on the invalids, it seemed.

"Is your head hurting?" Jessica asked.

"Not much. Why?"

"You looked…"

He smiled as she obviously sought a kind word. "Like an ogre?" he suggested.

"Uh, sort of."

Her answering smile caused his heart to jump up and down and generally make a fool of itself.

"Dinner," Violet called.

Clyde rose, careful not to jar his head with any sudden moves, and held out a hand to Jessica. He led her to the patio table and placed her beside him. He brushed the hair off her injured shoulder and subdued the impulsive urge to kiss her there.

When they'd left the hospital, Jessica had handled the horde of reporters with an aplomb that spoke of long experience in dealing with the media. She truthfully answered the questions shouted at them, but kept her replies short.

Somehow he and Smoky became the heroes of her tale. It had been damned embarrassing to admit the truth—that he'd only mopped up the operation. Jessica and Smoky had already weakened the stalker by the time he arrived on the scene.

While he found the reporters annoying, the microphones thrust beneath Jessica's nose and the TV lights shining in her eyes didn't faze her at all. Her smiling face and bright blue eyes had been beamed into every household in America on prime-time newscasts, along with his scowl and Violet's calm manner. Some of the newsmen had even managed to get a shot of Smoky lying bandaged and unconscious at the vet's office.

Violet gave Miles some instructions at the grill, then added some spices to the food. His sister hadn't examined him, but Clyde had been aware of her thoughtful gaze checking him out during the afternoon and evening.

He knew there was no brain damage, but heart damage? That was another story.

If Jessica had been hurt...

The thought was so painful, he had to divert his attention elsewhere. "That looks delicious," he told the cooks when he and Jessica were served helpings of grilled trout with seasoned rice.

He ate and joined in the conversation about the recent excitement. "What happens in the mind of someone like

Balter to make him think he owns another person?" he asked. He glanced at his sister.

She spread her hands in a helpless gesture. "I wish we knew. Are sociopaths born or made? Are their brains mis-wired, or is the lack of nurturing the problem?"

"Some of both, I think," Steven suggested.

Violet nodded. "There are no simple answers."

Clyde studied Jessica surreptitiously. She ate with her right hand, but moved her shoulder as little as possible due to the knife wound.

He knew he had to stop thinking about her getting killed, but the images of her fighting for her life buzzed around his restless mind like angry bees. When the meal was finally over and the bridal couple left with assurances that he and Jessica would be able to make the wedding, Violet shooed him and Jessica into the house and told them to go to bed.

"I'll bring you some warm milk and cookies later," she promised with a droll smile.

Upstairs, he pulled on a pair of sweats, then waited until he thought Jessica had had enough time to change.

When he knocked at her door and entered at her invitation, he found he'd timed it right. She was in bed.

She closed the thick biography and laid it on the bed-side table before modestly covering her night attire with the sheet. Her questioning glance was friendly but remote.

He sat on the side of the bed and immediately felt the warmth of her body through the layers of material that separated them. She moved over so they didn't touch.

"I have a question," he began.

She nodded, her lovely face composed and serious.

"When you saw the rose on your pillow, you didn't think of Balter putting it there, did you?"

That she was surprised at the question was obvious.

She hesitated, shook her head and immediately winced as the movement sent pain through her shoulder. He could identify with the feeling.

"I could kill him for that," he said, fierceness rising in him.

"He's behind bars," she said softly. "That's where he belongs."

"And you? Where do you belong?"

Her blue eyes flicked to him, then away. She laughed. "Have I outlasted my welcome? I'm very aware I've brought nothing but trouble with me on this visit. I'll leave tomorrow—"

"No," he said, taking her left hand and holding it between both of his. "That wasn't what I meant at all. Let's backtrack. What did you think when you saw the rose?"

"The one on my pillow?" Jessica asked, not at all ready to answer the question.

"Yes," he said with great patience, "the one on your pillow."

Sensing that he wasn't going to accept an evasive or flippant answer, she admitted, "I thought it could be from you, that it was your way of convincing me we should marry even though—"

She broke off, realizing she hadn't told him the rest of her news.

"What?" he said, sensing her hesitation.

"I haven't had a chance to tell you…" The words were harder to say than she'd thought they would be. She took a deep breath. "There isn't going to be a child."

"You aren't pregnant?"

She shook her head and felt an echo of sorrow inside, as if she'd lost something precious. "I never was."

"When did you know?"

"This morning, soon after I woke up. I discussed it with the doctor. He thought I was late due to the stress of Roy and fleeing the city and having to hide from him. It was probably the relief that the danger was over that triggered everything back to normal, physically."

"And mentally? Are you okay after the trauma?"

"Yes." She considered, then nodded firmly. "I really am, although it may take a while for my heart not to pound when I see roses."

She smiled at Clyde, then stopped when he gazed at her solemnly. His eyes went darker, and she wondered what he was thinking as he simply stared at her.

When he leaned forward slightly, her heart really did start pounding. Uncertainty and increasing tension caused it to skip a couple of beats.

They heard footsteps on the stairs. Clyde sighed and drew back. He smiled at his sister when she entered the room, but Jessica knew there was more he wanted to discuss.

"Here's your bedtime snack, as promised," she told them, a surprising gentleness in her voice and manner.

Jessica fought the sudden sting of tears. Everyone was being so kind. It rattled her composure. Maybe she wasn't as mentally calm, cool and collected as she thought.

After she and Clyde shared the snack, he left the room with his sister. Glad of a reprieve, Jessica brushed her teeth and went to bed.

She turned out the light, but found the dark disturbing. Flicking the lamp on to its lowest setting, she closed her eyes, sighed as a great weariness descended, and fell into a fretful sleep.

Even before Jessica opened her eyes, she knew something was different. Every nerve in her body jerked as she sat up and surveyed the room.

Flowers were everywhere. Roses. Dozens of them. In

vases on all the surfaces. Lying on the bed. In a trail of arrows leading out the door and into the gallery.

One perfect bud, just opening to disclose its pure red heart, was in a vase on the bedside table next to a glass of orange juice. Gingerly, due to her sore and very stiff shoulder, she sipped from the glass and studied the bud, then lifted it from the crystal container.

Not physically afraid, but filled with a wariness she couldn't ignore, she got out of bed and followed the trail of roses. It led to Clyde's door, which was partially open.

Slowly she pushed it back. No one was there, but rose petals covered the bed. She blinked in surprise.

Holding the single bud clutched to her bosom, she inhaled its delicate fragrance as if it were a form of courage and slowly stepped into the room. The door swung closed behind her.

"Oh," she said on a quickly drawn breath. A thorn pricked her finger. She stared at the drop of blood.

Clyde appeared and lifted her hand to his mouth to gently suck the tiny droplet away. "Sorry. I didn't have time to remove the thorns."

"You must have picked every rose in the garden."

He smiled. "Almost. I've been up since dawn."

"W-why?" She hoped he didn't hear the catch in her voice.

"Because I don't want you to be afraid when you see a rose on your pillow. I want you to think of me. As you did when you saw the other one."

Her mind was a total blank. She nodded, but she didn't understand anything about what was going on.

He led her to an easy chair. Once she was seated, he sat on the ottoman, their knees touching as he leaned close and took her hands. "I have something to say to you."

She wasn't sure she would be able to hear, her heart was beating that loud.

After a second of silence, he let out an audible breath. "Man, this is hard. I should have asked Steven for advice."

"Steven?" she said.

"Forget it. Flowers are supposed to have messages. Do you understand what I'm telling you?" He peered intently at her as he gestured at the flower she held.

She hesitated, then shook her head.

"You're not going to cut me any slack here, are you?"

"Uh, I don't think so." She needed words and vows, then maybe a lot of kisses and hugs before she accepted what his eyes were saying.

"I want the marriage," he said. "I want the kids. Most of all, I want you…for my wife, for my life's companion." He paused, then added, "For my love."

Her mind went hazy. She could only stare at him.

He cupped her face between his hands and delved into her eyes with his intense stare. "When I realized you were in danger…when you were running for your life and that madman was coming after you, and I could hardly get my legs to carry me, I realized how hollow my life would be without you in it. If you were killed…I never want to live through that again. I don't want to live without you."

She heard the individual words, but it took a moment for their meaning to come clear.

"I love you," he said. "I need the words from you. If you feel the same," he ended, sounding almost humble.

A brilliant light flooded her soul, illuminating all the longings of her wildly beating heart. When she opened her mouth, the words came out effortlessly, as if they'd been there all the time, waiting for their chance. "I love you," she whispered. "So much, so very, very much."

He lifted her onto his lap and folded her ever so carefully against his chest. "I wish I'd realized all this before you were nearly killed."

Happiness bubbled up in her. "But think what an exciting story we'll have to tell our children." She narrowed her eyes as if peering into some strange nether world. "It was a dark and stormy night—"

"There was a sliver of moonlight," he said in his serious way, "and we didn't have a storm."

"Who's telling this story?" she demanded, struggling to hold in laughter.

He gave her a sexy perusal. "Cut to the ending—the part where they kiss and live happily ever after. Like this."

When his lips touched hers, she was ready for him. She gave back passion for passion, caress for caress, kiss for kiss. Until they were breathless. Until they didn't need air, but only each other.

Finally he groaned and pulled back. "I can't make love to you," he complained. "My head is pounding like someone took a sledgehammer to it."

"Actually, it was a ballpeen hammer," she corrected in the sweetest tones. "I fell over it at the bottom of the stairs. I should have picked it up and whacked Roy on the head. Only I didn't think of it at the time."

Clyde pulled her to her feet. "Let's go tell Miles and Violet. We'll surprise them. Well, maybe not." He chuckled and tucked her against his side as they went down the steps to tell the world they were getting married.

Friday dawned with a crispness in the air that hinted at cooler months to come.

Jessica yawned, then lifted the one tiny rosebud on the pillow next to her and sniffed its dewy aroma. She was alone in the bed in the guest suite of the Flying Aces Ranch.

It was the last time she would be there as a guest.

Today was Steven and Amy's wedding day. It was also hers and Clyde's. When the other couple learned of their plans to marry as soon as possible, they had insisted on sharing the ceremony. Yesterday had been spent in planning the big surprise for their collective parents, family members and friends, arranging the marriage license and asking the pastor of the church in Red Rock to perform the second ceremony for her and Clyde.

Her soon-to-be husband.

She pressed a hand to her chest. So much happiness coming on the heels of so much terror might prove too much for her overactive heart.

Hearing voices downstairs, she hurriedly rose and dressed and went to join her beloved and her best friend for breakfast.

Later, Violet and Leslie helped her dress in her mother's wedding gown. Since Jessica was taller than anyone in her family, the dress was ballerina length on her and a little loose up top. Leslie, used to dealing with bridal problems, produced two bra inserts.

Jessica commented on Clyde's likely surprise at her sudden endowment. "He once said that along with my Texas twang, I was skinny enough to be a guitar string."

"No, no," Violet declared. "That was one of the cowboys from the Double Crown. I had a terrible crush on him until then. His comment made me so mad, I wouldn't speak to him after that. Poor guy, he never knew what he did wrong."

Clyde, dressed in a dark suit, paused in his pacing and listened to the laughter of the three women. "What do you think is so funny?" he asked his brother.

Miles, who was to be Clyde's best man, grinned and shrugged.

Clyde glanced at the kitchen clock and resumed pacing. "We're going to be late."

"Nah," Miles assured him.

"Okay, we're ready," Violet shouted down from the gallery rail. "You guys go on. We'll follow."

Clyde started to object, but Miles took his arm in a firm grip and led him out to the truck, which was mysteriously clean inside and out. So was the station wagon parked next to it. And the two sheriff's cruisers in the driveway.

"What the heck?" he said.

Miles laughed. "Come on. We can't keep the governor of Texas waiting. The man's on a tight schedule."

With a fore and aft police escort, the group arrived in style at the small church in Austin. The women were whisked through one door while the men were directed to another.

The ache in Clyde's head had dimmed to a dull echo, and he was impatient to claim his bride and take her home. He paused to reflect on the feeling. He'd expected the anticipation, but not the sense of responsibility, the need to blend his life with hers…and the tenderness, a vast ocean of it ebbing and flowing through him like the very tide of life itself.

Steven, with his best man, Ryan Fortune, entered the small antechamber, alongside the two ministers who would be performing the ceremony for each couple. The men shook hands.

"Jack and our parents are here," Steven said. "Their plane was delayed, so it was late when they got in last night. The governor has arrived too, along with the press and about a hundred TV crews."

"Ready?" the pastor of the church asked after peering into the auditorium and getting a nod from the organist.

The men entered and lined up before the bank of flowers in front of the altar. The church was standing-room-only.

Clyde's throat closed with a solid lump when the two brides, escorted by their fathers, came down the aisle. He recalled the stormy day when he'd picked Jessica up at the airport. He felt that now, at last, they'd reached the end of their journey.

When her father gave her over to his keeping, he felt he'd been given a treasure. Gazing into her beautiful, shining eyes, he knew he had.

"Dearly beloved," the minister began.

Steven and Amy said their vows.

"Dearly beloved," the second minister repeated.

Clyde and Jessica exchanged their vows.

The newlywed couples kissed as tradition required, then turned to the gathering of family and friends. A cheer from the crowd, as spontaneous as it was joyful, filled the air.

Steven and Clyde glanced at each other, then at Miles. "You're next," they said in unison.

"Horrors," he said as the bridal parties laughed in pure delight.

* * * * *

Everything you love about romance...
and more!

Please turn the page for Signature Select™
Bonus Features.

Bonus Features:

Signature Select™

BONUS FEATURES

Lone Star Rancher

EXCLUSIVE BONUS FEATURES INSIDE

Author Interview

A conversation with
LAURIE PAIGE

Recently, USA TODAY bestselling author Laurie Paige chatted with us as she took a break from writing her latest Silhouette Special Edition.

4

Tell us a bit about how you began your writing career.

My sister and I used to write two-page stories (mostly about animals and their adventures on our farm) and read them to each other when we were in elementary school. That started a lifelong love of reading. After growing up—college, working, marriage, motherhood—I read a romance novel, loved it and started writing my own stories again, this time about people.

Was there a particular person, place or thing that inspired this story?

I lived in Austin, Texas, at one time and my next-door neighbor was a native Texan. She told me about her ancestors who settled in the area—stories rich in history and adventure. I also traveled the state from border to border. The Pedernales cascades was a favorite day hike. LBJ's ranch was downriver from there.

What's your writing routine?
I am definitely a morning person. I get up around 6:30 a.m. and am usually at the desk around 7:30. I do original writing until lunchtime. Afternoons are devoted to chores and/or hiking the many logging trails in the area. In the evenings, I often read over what I've written that morning and do editing; the next morning I put in the changes and this gets me back into the story.

How do you research your stories?
I love interesting names on maps, so when we travel on vacations, I direct my husband to little-known roads. We stop at ghost towns and old graveyards. I also tend to accost ranchers, park rangers, librarians, waiters and anyone else who crosses my path with dozens of questions about the area. It amazes me that they answer and add in all kinds of useful details!

How you do develop your characters?
Some writers make lists about their characters, detailing schools, friends, hobbies and events in their lives. I like discovering things about my hero/heroine the same way we learn things about new friends—as they talk to each other or think about their life experiences, then I share these

tidbits with the reader. Writing their stories becomes a tale of discovery for me, too.

When you're not writing, what are your favorite activities?
Reading, of course. All kinds of books. Lots of ideas spring from this. I love exploring new places, so we travel quite a bit. Hiking is an exercise of mind and body. I find characters coming to life and story lines opening up as I tramp around the woods or a nearby lake. Hiking is also a social outlet. I belong to a weekly hiking group. We usually hike to some lovely viewpoint and eat lunch, then hike back. Occasionally after a hike, we meet at someone's home and have a cookout or ice-cream party, sometimes a wine tasting since one member of the group is a vintner. Gardening is a newly discovered pleasure. We also get together with family and friends every holiday. I usually save some bulbs and seeds for fall planting, so at Thanksgiving everyone helps with this. At spring break, we admire our handiwork as daffodils, tulips, crocuses and lilies come up.

If you don't mind, could you tell us a bit about your family?
I was the youngest of seven children, which is rather akin to growing up with four extra fathers and two extra mothers as everyone feels free to boss the baby! Our farm in Kentucky seemed a magical place to me. I roamed all over it, rode the two horses, and also tried riding the milk cows and the pigs. Did you

know pigs buck just like horses? Neighbors would get together nearly every Saturday night and have square dances at each other's homes. Everyone would bring a dish or two, plus dessert. When we moved to town, I found that was lots of fun, too. My family attended the Baptist church, where I belonged to the choir. I also went to choir at the Methodist church, story hour at a nearby Presbyterian church and art class at the Christian church. Best of all were the library and museum, only five blocks away and a short detour from school to home. Growing up, I always had a dog (and still do). The first book I ever owned was *Heidi*. My favorite book is still *The Little Engine That Could*.

What are your favorite kinds of vacations? Where do you like to travel?
I love vacations with family and friends, the more the merrier. We have visited all fifty states...or fifty-one, as we in Northern California like to say. There was actually a movement in the late 1800s to establish the state of Jefferson, carved out of Northern California and southern Oregon. Today we have road signs declaring Scenic Highways, put up by the state of Jefferson and local radio stations with this name. Last year my sister, brother-in-law, husband and I visited presidential homes and civil war battlegrounds in Virginia, Pennsylvania and other points back East. Another year we traveled across Canada. With friends, we camped in all the national parks of the western U.S. and Canada.

We've hiked sections of the Pacific Crest Trail (and have a friend who has hiked the whole thing!). This past summer, we visited all the caves we came across during a trip to Kentucky for a family reunion. Cruising is a new discovery. We "did" Alaska and the Panama Canal and would like to try diving in the Caribbean. Five of us went Down Under and explored Australia from coast to coast. The three-day trip from Perth to Sydney by train was fun and relaxing; the Aussies were great hosts. So were the Kiwis when we toured New Zealand, staying in private B and Bs in people's homes. While I enjoy new landscapes, I love meeting the residents more. People are endlessly fascinating!

Do you have a favorite book or film?
I've mentioned *The Little Engine That Could*. And *Heidi*. In science fiction, *The Mote in God's Eye* is an all-time favorite. In romance/women's fiction, there are too many to name. For films, who can forget *Gone with the Wind*? The old aunts never appreciated Scarlett, but Melanie knew who kept the wolf (or carpetbaggers) from the door. Scarlett had her flaws but, for me, she was like the little engine— she kept going no matter what life threw at her. And there's that great five-hankie movie, *An Affair To Remember*. Oh, and *Madame X* with Lana Turner. I used to wait up for my husband, who worked second shift at the Kennedy Space Center at the time, and it seemed *Madame X* was on once a week.

By the time I saw it the third time, I was crying from the opening credits....

Any last words to your readers?
Like all readers, I love entering the world of heroes and heroines in the stories. I laugh with them. I cry with them. I sometimes frown on their decisions, but as long as I understand why they did what they did, I'm okay with that. I think stories can be great learning tools. They can also heal. While working in the school library, the librarian once told me she could always tell the students who came from difficult homes. They wanted sad stories that "come out happy at the end." I like that for my characters, too, and for the readers who turn to stories for pleasure, to escape from everyday life for a few hours and sometimes to heal a heart that's been trampled.

Don't miss Laurie Paige's Silhouette Special Edition, *The Other Side of Paradise,* available in September 2005.

LAURIE PAIGE'S

Travel Tale...

Everyone has a travel tale...an adventure experienced while on vacation or while on a business trip. Laurie Paige shares with us her travelogue of her trip across Texas. 🖎

10 Texas in Eight Days, Twice

When we moved from Satellite Beach, Florida, to Austin, Texas, we took the scenic route by way of Kentucky to attend family reunions. Since my husband, Bob, and I are from the same hometown, our families cooperate so we have one reunion on a Saturday and one on a Sunday. After a fun, but hectic, visit, we head for Texas on a rather erratic trail to take in as much of the state as possible. I have an atlas and a Texas map in hand so we can explore places with interesting/unusual names. This is my favorite method of getting story ideas.

One thing I notice right away is that most of the rivers flow southeast into the Gulf of Mexico.

From sea level at the barrier islands along the eastern coast, the land rises to its highest point at maybe a hundred miles from El Paso. Hmm, there's a Colorado River here as well as in the Far West; it flows through Austin, our destination. Also a Red River. I think every state must have a Red River. The one in Texas is on its northern border and separates the state from Oklahoma. The Red runs into the Mississippi River rather than the gulf.

From the Louisiana-Texas border heading due west to El Paso, Texas is one-third of the distance across the U.S. at this point. It's nearly as "tall" as all the states north of it up to the Canadian border. No wonder our Texan heroes think big!

The humidity along the Gulf coast doesn't faze us. It's the same as Florida. We often have afternoon rains as we wander along the coast from Caddo, a scenic park in the bayou region along the Louisiana border (think *Evangeline* and Spanish moss) to Corpus Christi. We try out all the different seafood dishes we can find: gumbo, blackened seabass, crayfish. I learn file powder is made from dried okra. Yum!

We arrive at Austin, our destination and new home. First of all, I get locked out of my car at the grocery on my way to meet the movers. I call 911, but am informed this is not an emergency. (Ask my cat, who's locked in the car!) However, a policeman arrives and calls a locksmith. In twenty minutes I'm on my way to the new house. I'm going to name a hero after each of them.

Once settled in, I go exploring. The Pedernales Falls west of town are a long stretch of lovely cascades along the river with rocks scoured smooth by the water. I find a cave carved into the limestone and immediately start thinking of story ideas. The LBJ Ranch is on the Pedernales. Bob and I drive by and continue on to Fredericksburg, settled by German immigrants, where we eat delicious frankfurters with sauerkraut and cheese, one of my hubby's favorite meals.

The surprising thing about the Alamo is that it is in the middle of town in San Antonio, surrounded by traffic and tall buildings. I'm not sure what I expected—a large park around it, or perhaps a fort on a hill that overlooks the town. The bustle and noise are soon forgotten as we explore the mission and the barracks. A sense of history and a connection with the past shape my thoughts and feelings as I realize I'm standing where Davy Crockett and Jim Bowie once stood! Also John Wayne had been there. His picture was on a wall.

A few weeks pass before we are able to range farther afield. On a weekend drive, traveling a county road, we meander deep into the heart of Texas Hill Country. At one point, I realize that other than the road, which started out paved but is now gravel and hardly more than one lane wide, and a fence on each side, there is no sign of human habitation—no houses, no other cars on the road, no barns, just rolling hills and sagebrush as far as the eye can see. I feel like the loneliest person in the world. The road goes to one barely discernible track, then two ruts. We bravely carry on. Until we come to a cattle guard over a culvert. The road disappears, apparently onto someone's ranch, although there are no signs to indicate this other than a cattle skull nailed to a fence post. We take this as an omen to turn back...and we do, beating a hasty retreat to Austin and home, which takes four hours.

That summer the temperature hits 110 degrees. I sit in the kiddie pool at the park and read most afternoons. Pecan trees are filled with developing nuts. I vow to collect a bunch in October.

This was not to be. The squirrels beat me to the draw. As compensation, we take a week to trek into the Far West. Traveling by scenic Highway 377, we mosey into Del Rio and I wade in the Rio Grande. The Rio Grande! The Real One! The water comes about halfway up to my knees. I study the banks and wonder how deep the river once was before we started irrigation projects. From the other side of the river, three men and two women also wade into the water. We smile and nod as they pass. They soon disappear from sight. My dear heart thinks we should vamoose, too. Like the Western heroes of movies, we ride into the sunset.

Big Bend National Park goes on my list of favorite places to "get away from it all." We camp in its quiet canyons among limestone cliffs and cedar trees. A nosy coyote sneaks into our camping site and sniffs around. He doesn't notice me sitting on a nearby boulder, hardly daring to breathe as I observe him. After five minutes, not finding anything of interest, he looks directly at me, then trots off with his tail set in a distinctly disdainful attitude.

The land west of the Pecos River is the southern end of the Rocky Mountains. The elevation rises from 1500 feet at the Rio Grande Valley to the highest point of Texas, Guadalupe Peak in Culberson County. Yep, definitely what I would call rugged country. We travel along Highway 90, then I-10 to El Paso. I watch for scenes of ranching life and roundups.

El Paso! City of song and legend! Shootouts and badlands! Cowboys! At last!

Oh, they're filming a movie. There are semitrailers and cables all over the place. We join a crowd of sightseers, but no one knows what film or actors are involved. I ask a camera crewman and he tells me it's a TV commercial for laundry detergent. Huh, moms already know everything about stains and spots. I check out the town, the river and some mines in the wilds of the desert, or plains, as they call them.

Going north we are awed by the soft hues of the Llano Estacado, or Staked Plains, all subtle yellows and reds, their layers exposed by erosion. The plains rise to more than 4000 feet and are level, except where cut by deep arroyos, dry now, but dangerous in a sudden storm, as we are warned by the owner of a grocery/gas station sitting like a lone sentinel at a crossroads. The land reminds me of Australia's outback—very few trees and a sparse growth of coarse grasses, unless irrigated. Again we hit a stretch where we see no other signs of life, unless you count the dead armadillo beside the road. Rain is also sparse, less than ten inches per year. Unused to the low humidity, we get minor nosebleeds; we keep water and iced tea in hand constantly.

We pass through Lubbock with its oil wells and Amarillo with its cattle yards. We had to hold our breaths a couple of times when the wind was in our direction as we passed the feed lots filled with a mixture of cattle, but otherwise found it all fascinating. One thing we found everywhere we went—jalapeños: on pizzas, in corn bread, cooked in chili and brown beans and soup. After a week, I can eat them without weeping.

We follow the Brazos to Waco, visiting a prairie-dog town on the way, then pick up I-35 and are soon in Austin and home.

HOME ON THE RANGE
by Elizabeth Bevarly
(Part 2 of a 3–part serial)

CHAPTER 4

Megan instinctively lurched forward at the sound of gunfire…then realized belatedly that the only place to land was against Nash Ridley's broad chest. Worse—oh, all right, maybe better—the moment she made contact, he instinctively wrapped his sturdy arms around her.

Strangely, though, when he did that, all the fear she'd felt dissolved completely. Because she was too busy noticing instead the firm, masculine flesh beneath her fingertips, and the warm breath stirring the hair at her temples and the sudden pounding of her heart.

She glanced up to find Nash gazing down at her, and he looked as surprised as she felt. Though whether that was because of the sudden gunshot or, like Megan, the sudden zinging of the strings of his heart, she couldn't have said. She only knew that the way he was looking at her and the way she was feeling about him changed a lot in that instant.

Then, at the far fringes of her mind, she heard the

sound of laughter, and it dawned on her that maybe what she had heard hadn't been a gunshot at all. Or that there was a reason for it that everyone else understood but she and Nash had missed. Or maybe everyone was laughing at her and Nash, and the cowardly way she'd reacted to what must have been a harmless sound.

Looking up, she saw everyone looking at another ranch hand who was holding a dead rabbit, his rifle propped proudly against his shoulder.

"Got yer dinner for ya, Clyde!" the man called out as everyone's laughter doubled. "I'll see if I can't find a couple more for Steven and Miles, too!"

Megan felt a momentary rush of relief, but when she realized she was still in Nash Ridley's arms—and that neither of them was doing anything to change that—she tensed again. But it wasn't the kind of tension that came with anxiety and fear. It was the kind that came with anticipation and excitement…and not a little pleasure.

"Looks like rabbit's on the menu for dinner at the big house tonight."

Nash murmured the observation in a very quiet voice very close to Megan's ear, and she felt an involuntary shudder wind through her body. She told herself it was due to the sight of the dead animal dangling from the cowboy's hand. But she knew that wasn't it.

There was a ripple of pleasure mixed with it, and that could only be because of Nash's nearness, and the gentle way he was touching her. His fingers raked lightly over her bare arms, as if he were trying to soothe her fears. But there was too much intimacy in the touch for it to be simply reassuring. And there was something else, too, something she'd probably be better off not thinking about. Because she was only going to be in Red Rock for a week, and Nash was ten years younger than she, and they had nothing in common, and it felt much too good, having this stranger so close.

"Not for me," she said. And for a minute, she couldn't remember what she was talking about, what it was that wasn't for her. Besides Nash Ridley, she meant. Then she remembered the cowboy holding the dead rabbit, and she shivered again. She looked back at Nash, whose warm fingers still stroked up and down her bare arms, and who she couldn't quite bring herself to tell "Stop that." Instead, she told him, "I don't want to eat anything I've personally seen murdered. You can have my share."

He shook his head. "No thanks," he said. "I'm a vegetarian."

Megan would have been less surprised if he'd told her he was wearing women's underwear. "Are you serious?" she said before she could stop herself.

He smiled curiously. "What? You never heard of a vegetarian cowboy?"

"Well, no," she said. "I thought red meat was a staple for you guys. I mean there are all those wide-open range, sweeping Aaron Copeland score, manly man commercials for beef."

He lifted a shoulder and let it drop. And continued to brush his fingers along her very sensitive flesh. "That's just a stereotype perpetuated by shortsighted advertising executives who can't come up with an original idea."

Megan felt herself coloring at that, but had no idea what to say.

"What?" he asked, his smile growing broader. "You never heard of someone whose job is to convince people to give up their hard-earned dollars in exchange for some idealized state of mind that only exists on a television screen or the pages of a glossy magazine?"

Megan made herself smile back at him, but knew it was sheepishly. "Um, yeah," she said. "Me."

Nash's smile fell. "What?"

"What you just described is what I do for a living," she told him, realizing the comment held more than a grain of truth. The campaigns she created for LA Mode were pretty much designed to do exactly what he said—make people buy into an image that she and her colleagues fabricated. "I'm the creative director of an advertising company in Los Angeles."

This time Nash was the one whose face colored. "Oh."

Somehow, though, Megan couldn't find it in herself to get angry. He was essentially right, after all. And neither his tone of voice nor he himself had been condemning or accusatory when he offered his assessment of her profession. He'd simply been voicing an observation he'd made.

And between that and the vegetarian thing, she realized he was in no way the stereotypical cowboy that she'd decided he must be—the stereotypical cowboy she might very well have used in a campaign.

How very interesting.

She also realized that the two of them were still standing with their arms around each other—mostly because she heard Miles call out with a laugh, "Knock off the kissy face, you two, and get to work!" She made herself drop her hands back to her sides and take a few steps in retreat.

Immediately, she felt uncomfortable, a reaction she told herself was crazy. She barely knew this guy. She should have been uncomfortable standing so close to him while his warm fingers drifted over her bare skin. But that hadn't been the case at all.

"We better saddle up," Nash said, "and get a move on. Everyone else is on their way."

"Saddle up?" Megan said, confused. "I thought we'd be driving."

Nash looked past her and shook his head. "All the trucks are either gone or have people in them. You and I are going to be on horse patrol."

Horse patrol? Megan repeated to herself. Why would Steven put her on a horse? He knew she didn't like to ride. He knew that when they were kids, she'd done just about anything to avoid riding. But there was a good reason for that, Megan knew, even if she'd never told any of her cousins about it.

Megan was terrified of horses. Terrified. *Terr. I. Fied.* And now Nash Ridley was going to make her climb on top of one.

22

CHAPTER 5

Nash stood in the Fortunes' main barn looking at Megan, certain he must have misunderstood what she'd just told him. But then, he couldn't mishear something like *I'm terrified of horses. Terrified. Terr. I. Fied.*

It was kind of hard to miss her point.

"How can you be scared of a horse?" he asked. Hell, it made more sense to be scared of a lace tablecloth. After all, you could spill something on a lace tablecloth and get yelled at by your stepmom. He should know. To this day, he was in no way comfortable around tatting of any kind. "Horses are harmless."

"They're big," Megan said. "And they have teeth. Big teeth. And they bite."

"They only bite people who are asking for it," Nash said. "A nice lady like you, you won't have any problem."

"Hah," Megan scoffed. "And again, I say, hah. And in case I didn't mention it, hah."

Nash shook his head. Not only was Misty, the old gray mare Steven had told him to put Megan on, the gentlest creature to ever come down the pike, but Nash wasn't even sure how many teeth the animal still had. He'd certainly never known the horse to bite anyone. Even people who deserved it.

"Misty is the sweetest horse you'll ever meet," he told Megan. "Trust me."

She eyed him dubiously and reiterated, "Hah."

"Steven told me you know how to ride," Nash said, taking another tack. "He said you used to ride all the time when y'all were kids."

"I do know how to ride," Megan assured him. "I just don't want to. Ever again. For the rest of my natural life."

Well, that was pretty specific, Nash thought. And then, suddenly, he understood. The only reason people who'd ridden as kids stopped riding for the rest of their natural lives was because they had a bad experience at some point that made them wary of ever getting back on a horse again.

"It's got nothing to do with big teeth and biting," he said. "You got thrown real bad once, didn't you?"

Her mouth flattened into a tight line, but she nodded.

"Darlin', that happens to even the most experienced riders every now and then. It's nothing to be ashamed of."

"It didn't make me ashamed," she said quickly—

and, he had to admit, without an ounce of shame. "It made me terrified. *Terrified. Terr. I. Fied.*"

"So you've said."

"Well, if you heard me say it, then why do you keep carping on it?"

"Because it's stupid, that's why," he told her. "Now come here."

She thrust out her lower lip mutinously, and Nash nearly laughed out loud. "Please," he qualified belatedly. "Come here."

She stuffed her hands into her back pockets defiantly, but took enough steps forward to be standing beside Nash in front of Misty's stall.

"Megan Lavery," he said, "I'd like you to meet Misty, uh, Gray. Misty Gray, meet Megan Lavery."

The horse, at least, had some sense of courtesy, because she ambled over to the stall door and softly whinnied a greeting. Megan at least didn't bolt in the opposite direction, which Nash had halfway expected. But neither did she extend a hand to the animal, as polite manners dictated.

Nash reached out his own hand and wrapped his fingers lightly around hers. Then, noting only a small reluctance on her part to withdraw it when she realized his intention, he began to guide it toward the horse's head.

"I don't—" she began.

But she never finished whatever she'd intended to say. Which was just as well, because Nash wasn't listening anyway, on account of his body started to malfunction the second he touched her. Heat fizzled through him as if he'd suffered a short circuit in his wiring, and his brain went completely on the fritz. But that was nothing compared to the buzzing that erupted in his ears or the shock wave that shuddered through his entire system.

Damn, he thought. If that was what happened just touching her hand, what would it do to him if he touched—

He halted the thought right there before completing the thought. Somehow, he knew even thinking about touching some other body part than the ones that were readily accessible would make him spontaneously combust.

Forcing himself to focus on the matter at hand… Uh, what was it again…? Oh, yeah. Getting Megan comfortable with Misty. Forcing himself to focus on that, he guided her hand to the mare's velvety muzzle and cupped her fingers over it. The horse whinnied softly again, bumping her nose lightly against Megan's fingers. Nash grinned when he saw Megan's smile.

"See there?" he said. "She's gentle as a lamb."

"*Silence of the Lambs,* maybe," Megan muttered.

But he could see she was softening toward the creature. He let her get comfortable with the mare, listened while she talked to Misty and even leaned forward to nuzzle noses with her, until she finally relented and agreed that okay, if she had to, she could probably get on a horse again and ride, even though it had been years, and Nash better not laugh at her or else she'd kick him in the shins. He laughed as she complained, and bantered playfully with her, thinking he hadn't had this much fun with a woman for a long time.

Together, they led Misty out to the corral, and together they saddled her up. Megan commented that riding a horse was like riding a bicycle—you never really forgot how—then mounted the mare like an expert.

"How long did you say it's been since you rode?" he asked as she adjusted herself on the saddle, getting her balance.

"Oh, gosh, probably twenty years or so," she said. "Not since before I learned to drive."

Nash was reminded of how much older she was than him, but he'd be damned if he felt a single one of the years between them. He'd been on his own since he left home at sixteen after his father had taken off with wife number four, something that had matured him pretty quickly. And Megan had a playful streak in her that shaved quite a bit off her own age. All in all, he figured they pretty well met somewhere in the middle.

He wondered what would happen if they met somewhere else.

That hot feeling starting simmering in his midsection again, so he pushed the thought away and led Misty and Megan around the corral for a few minutes. Then he let Megan take over on her own while he saddled his own horse, a gelding named Buck he'd bought himself for his twenty-first birthday.

He was about to lift the saddle onto Buck's back when he heard a sound everyone in this part of Texas recognized, but which no one ever wanted to hear: the shake, clatter and roll of a rattlesnake. And it was way too close for comfort.

"Um, Nash?"

He knew before he even turned around that Megan had heard it, too, but it was only when he'd completed the rotation that he realized she also saw it. Because he saw it then, too, coiled up in a patch of sunlight near the fence—less than a foot away from where Misty, who'd also obviously seen it now, came to a halt.

28

Before Nash or Megan could do anything, the horse took matters into her own hands. With a toss of her head and an unholy shriek, she rose on her hind legs and pawed violently at the air. Then she came down on all fours again and bolted. As fast as she could. Right through the open gate of the corral. Jerking her reins from Megan's hands.

Who, Nash could see as she disappeared, was clinging to the animal's mane for dear life.

CHAPTER 6

As the wind screeched through Megan's hair and the horse beneath her bucked and shimmied, one thought and one alone circled through her head: *Gentle as a lamb my aunt Fanny.*

In less than a nanosecond, Misty had gone from *mild thing* to *wild thang,* and Megan had no idea what to do—short of panicking. She'd been so surprised by the appearance of the snake and Misty's violent reaction to it that she hadn't been prepared when the animal lurched and bolted, and the reins had been stripped right out of her hands. At the moment, they were flapping in the wind too far from her reach, so she gripped Misty's mane with both fists and held on.

Think, Megan, think, she instructed herself. And, just like that, she went into executive mode. Which meant no panicking allowed. Which meant reasoning this thing out.

She wrapped Misty's mane around her fingers, clenched her legs tight around the horse's middle and reminded herself that she'd ridden bareback before, when she was very young, even if it hadn't been at great speed. And Misty was eating up ground faster than Megan drove on the 405. Of course, the 405 was generally clogged with traffic, but that was beside the point. The point was that if Megan didn't do something quickly, she—and Misty—would be back in L.A. a lot sooner than she'd planned.

And strangely, in spite of her current situation, she realized she didn't want to return to L.A. just yet. No, she wanted to stay in Red Rock long enough to… Wow, she marveled when she realized where the thought was going. Long enough to get to know Nash Ridley a little—no, *a lot*—better, which she wouldn't be able to do unless she did something to stop Misty's mad dash.

Forcing herself to remain calm, she tried everything she could think to do to slow the horse's speed, but Misty would not be slowed. She was a spry little thing for her age, and evidently had rattlesnake issues even worse than Megan's horse issues. So Megan clung to the beast with her fists and her knees as well as she could and waited for Misty to tire.

She had no idea how long or far the mare had been running when Nash finally drew up alongside both of them on his big, buff-colored horse, but their arrival calmed Misty down immediately.

She slowed enough that Nash was able to pass her, then gently guide her to slowing even more. Eventually, she trotted to a stop, shaking her head, gasping for breath and making frightened little horsey sounds.

Megan immediately leaped to the ground. Nash followed, gathering both horses' reins in one hand before striding over to where she stood, bent with her hands braced on her knees, reacting much like Misty, save the horsey sounds. Although, her breathing did sound a little off....

"Guess the old gray mare just ain't what she used to be, huh?" Nash asked with a grin.

Miraculously, Megan controlled the urge to smack him upside the head. Instead, she said between breaths, "As God is my witness...I will never...get on a horse...ever again...for the rest of my...natural...life."

"I dunno," Nash said. "You did awfully well for someone who's *terr-i-fied* of horses. I'm thinkin' maybe they don't scare you as much as you thought. I'm thinkin' maybe you'd do all right, if, say...you had to work on a ranch or something."

She narrowed her eyes at him, but for some reason found herself reluctant to disagree with him. She told herself it was because she didn't want to argue with him. Somehow, though, she didn't think that was quite it. "Well, then, I'm not getting on a horse again today," she qualified.

"Okay," he said. "But that's gonna make the trip back to the Flying Aces a little longer than it needs to be. I think ol' Misty here covered a good mile or two before we got her stopped."

"No…problem," Megan said. "It's a…good day… for walking."

He looked up at the cloudy sky overhead. "Actually, it's not."

"The rain'll hold off for a little longer," she assured him, echoing Steven's earlier words.

But Nash had started shaking his head before Megan even finished talking. "Actually, I don't think it will," he told her.

She glanced up, too, and as if cued by his comment, a single, cold drop of rain splashed onto her face. Followed by another. Then another. And another.

"Dammit," she said.

32 He looked at her and smiled. "So then you're not one of those girls who likes piña coladas and gettin' caught in the rain, huh?"

"On the contrary. I could really go for a piña colada right now. Or, better still, a nice big shot of tequila."

He chuckled at that, then graduated to full blown laughter as the skies opened up and let loose with a downpour.

"Dammit," Megan said again, with more feeling this time.

Nash extended Misty's reins toward her silently, but Megan shook her head. She was not getting back on that horse for a while. Once burned, twice shy and all that. Twice burned and, well… Suffice it to say she was having uncharitable thoughts about a glue factory.

"I'll walk," she stated adamantly.

Nash shrugged. "Suit yourself."

And with that, he released both sets of reins and whistled out a command, and both horses took off at a trot in the direction of the Flying Aces. Obviously he intended to walk with her. Obviously, she didn't mind. She smiled at him through the rain, and he smiled back, and suddenly, she rather did like the thought of getting caught in the rain.

"You sure they'll be able to find their way back?"

He nodded. "Better than we will, probably."

"What do you mean?" she asked. "Don't you know where we are?"

"Pretty much," he told her.

"*Pretty* much?" she echoed.

"Well, I got a little frantic when Misty took off with you, and I didn't pay much attention to which way she headed—I just took off after her. And she zigged and zagged a lot, and since the sun's not out, and there are no trees out here to look for moss on…"

"Is that really true?" Megan asked, interrupting. "That you can figure out directions by looking at moss on a tree? I thought that was a myth."

He eyed her in silence for a minute, then reached out to run his fingers over her head, as if checking for bumps. "You sure you didn't take a spill at some point during that ride?" he asked. "You're not making much sense."

She started to duck out from under his hand, but something made her stop. Mostly the fact that she kind of liked the way it felt to have him touching her. So she only met his gaze levelly and said, "I'm fine. Just a little rattled."

Nash said nothing, just continued to stroke his hand gently over her now wet hair. But his gaze never left hers, and hers never left his, and for a minute, they only stood there in the rain staring at each other while he touched her and she wanted desperately to touch him.

Finally, when she couldn't stand it anymore, Megan lifted a hand and, after only a small hesitation, she moved her fingers to his mouth and ran them gently over his lower lip. He closed his eyes for a minute, and when he opened them again, his pupils were huge and dark and hungry.

"Rattled, huh?" he said softly. The hand on her hair moved back to her neck, and he closed his fingers around her warm nape. "Well, darlin', that makes two of us."

And before Megan realized what was happening, he was lowering his head to hers.

THE END

Want to read more? Look for the continuation of Home on the Range *in the bonus features of the next* THE FORTUNES OF TEXAS: REUNION *book,* The Good Doctor *by Karen Rose Smith, on sale October 2005.*

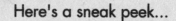

Here's a sneak peek...

THE GOOD DOCTOR
by
Karen Rose Smith

You won't want to miss the continuation of
THE FORTUNES OF TEXAS: REUNION, *a new
12-book continuity series featuring the powerful Fortune
family. Enjoy this excerpt of Karen Rose Smith's*
The Good Doctor, *the fifth book in the series—
available October 2005.*

SNEAK PEEK BONUS FEATURE

CHAPTER 1

"You've got it all now," Linda Clark decided as she appraised her brother.

"Just wait till those nurses get a gander at you," Stacey agreed, her smile as wide as her sister's.

Dr. Peter Clark swiftly closed his office door, hoping no one had heard. "Cool it, you two," he demanded in a stern voice as he strode to his desk, wondering how long this visit was going to last. He had an appointment in fifteen minutes. His sisters weren't in awe of him as some of his patients were, so it might be hard to kick them out. He loved them dearly but sometimes…

"I don't know why I let you dress me like a mannequin," he grumbled. He was still not sure the navy, tweed blazer was something he would have chosen on his own. He definitely wouldn't have bought the silk shirt and the patterned designer tie.

"You turned thirty-nine yesterday, and you wouldn't even let us give you a party. The least we could do is spruce you up a bit," Linda teased. "Now tall, dark and handsome really applies. I like the new haircut, and we didn't even have anything to do with *that*."

"My regular barber was out of town."

A laugh came from Stacey's direction. "Thank goodness!"

He'd had enough. They'd taken him to lunch and then accompanied him to a men's store to pick up his tuxedo for Friday night. Despite his protests, they'd insisted on buying him a blazer, shirt and tie as birthday gifts, convincing the store manager to have them pressed so he could wear the outfit back to the office.

He deliberately checked his watch. "I have an appointment in ten minutes."

38

"We're not leaving until you assure us you'll show up on Friday night."

Counting to five, he tried to keep the impatience from his voice. "You talked me into the bachelor auction because it's for a good cause. I never go back on my word. Not even if that means I have to endure the humiliation of standing on a runway and having women bid on me. Now, as I said…"

Linda sighed. "Your life is much too serious. I couldn't stand doing what you do. A pediatric neurosurgeon holds too much power in his hands. How do you handle that responsibility?"

"Very carefully," he replied seriously.

Nothing meant more to him than his work and the kids he treated. In fact there was one right now who was breaking his heart. The bachelor auction would be raising money for high-tech equipment for the pediatrics wing to help children like Celeste. That was the only reason he'd agreed to be a part of it. That, and the fact that the wing had been built as a memorial to his mother. If only there was someone like his mom to help with his little patient. She needed loving care as much as she needed high-tech equipment and surgery—maybe even more.

There was a knock on his office door and Katrina, his receptionist, poked her head inside. "Dr. Violet Fortune is here. I didn't think you'd want to keep her waiting."

"A Fortune coming to see you? What's all that about?" Linda asked. Then, as if a lightbulb went on in her head, she snapped her fingers. "Oh, I get it. Violet Fortune's a neurologist with a reputation almost as good as yours. Maybe she came all the way from New York to consult with you."

"Okay," Peter said, rising to his feet. "You did *not* hear a name. You have amnesia about anything Katrina said."

"We'll see Violet Fortune on our way out. Her picture has been in *The Red Rock Gazette* now and then," Linda concluded. "You know, that paper *you* never read because medical journals are more important."

Both of them were on their feet now, realizing he did have work to do. Linda gave him a quick hug. "Happy day-after-your-birthday once more." She patted the sleeve of his blazer. "Really hot," she kidded again.

He couldn't help but laugh then as Stacey hugged him, too, and added, "If not before, we'll see you Friday night. Just make sure that black tie's straight before you stroll down the runway, okay?"

When his sisters stepped into the hall, he decided to walk them out. He didn't want them waylaying Dr. Fortune out of curiosity. They must have sensed that because they grinned at him, waved and cast a few long glances at the woman sitting in his waiting room. Seconds later they were gone and he turned his attention to Violet Fortune.

As soon as he did, he was caught off-guard. She was stunning. Absolutely stunning. Her reputation as a brilliant diagnostician had already reached Texas. At only thirty-three, she'd already made her mark in her field. Maybe he'd envisioned her in a lab coat, with a severe hairdo and a no-nonsense demeanor, but the flesh-and-blood Violet Fortune was the polar opposite.

"Dr. Fortune?" he asked, just to make sure.

Standing, placing the magazine she'd been paging through on the chair beside her, she gave him a smile that socked him in the solar plexus. "Yes, I'm Dr. Fortune. Are you Dr. Clark?"

"Last time I looked," he countered with his own smile, ignoring the lightninglike signals his libido was sending his body.

When he extended his hand, the action helped him

focus and he could more easily ignore the reaction he was having to her. "It's good to meet you, although I'm a bit puzzled as to why you're here."

"Ryan and Lily have spoken highly of you."

The soft grip of her hand registered along with everything else about her. She seemed to be looking into his eyes with the same intensity he was looking into hers, and that created electricity.

"I think highly of them," he said, releasing her and pulling away.

Breaking eye contact, she quickly glanced around the office but no one else was in the room. Despite the fact his receptionist was behind her glass window, still Violet kept her voice low. "This visit has to do with Ryan."

All business now, hearing the somberness in her voice, he motioned down the hall. "Let's talk in my office."

Having decided long ago not to follow in any man's footsteps, Violet kept up with Peter's long strides, studying him while he didn't have his attention on her, wondering why the earth had seemed to shake a little when he'd taken her hand in his. She didn't react that way to men, especially not male doctors. Peter's tall, lean but muscular physique, his short but thick black hair and his piercing green eyes had created a twitter inside of her she couldn't seem to still.

His office door was open, and he stood aside so

she could enter before him. A gentleman, she thought.

The aroma of coffee wafted around the office and Peter gestured to the pot on the credenza that had obviously just been brewed. "Katrina must have snuck in here and started that for me. Would you like a cup?"

"No thanks. I'm fine." Violet was worried and anxious enough. She didn't need caffeine revving her up more. Maybe that was why she felt this attraction to Dr. Clark, because her guard was down. It had been down for over two months now. That was why she'd come to Texas to her brothers' ranch and answered Ryan's call.

42   Apparently deciding his own mug of coffee could wait, Peter Clark lowered himself into the high-back, leather swivel chair behind his desk. He waited until she'd seated herself in one of the gray tweed chairs across from it. The barrier and the bit of distance made her feel more self-possessed than when he'd greeted her in the reception area.

"So what can I do for you?" he asked, curiosity evident in his expression.

Taking her dark red clutch bag in her hands, she opened it and extracted a legal-sized envelope. When she handed it to him, she concluded seriously, "You'd better read this first. It's from Ryan."

After he glanced at it, he looked even more perplexed. "Essentially it's a release form giving you permission to discuss him with me."

She nodded. "That's precisely what it is. I'm not only a relative and good friend to Ryan and Lily, but I'm a neurologist, as well."

"I know that. I'm familiar with the articles you've published. You've made a name for yourself in a short amount of time."

"I guess New York isn't as far from Texas as I sometimes think it is."

"The world *is* getting smaller, but it's more than that. Red Rock is a small community and the Fortune name means something here. Besides your relationship to Ryan and Lily, your brothers have established themselves, too."

Her brothers Jack, Steven, Miles and Clyde had vacationed in Red Rock as kids and the latter three had decided to settle here as adults. Steven had bought his own ranch, Loma Vista, and was renovating it. A gala, during which the governor was going to present Ryan with an award, would take place there next month. Miles and Clyde's chicken ranch, the Flying Aces, where she was staying, was thriving. Her oldest brother, Jack, had just married recently and settled here, too.

"What I'm getting at," Peter continued, "is that the Fortunes are continuously discussed in Red Rock, and that includes you."

"Me? I don't even live here."

"No, but your name and career are bandied about along with all the other Fortunes. Most people in town know your history."

"What history would that be?"

"Education history for one thing. I heard with tutors you graduated high school a year early. You also did a four-year college program in three. In med school, you earned respect quickly and began seeing patients in New York City when you joined a prestigious neurological practice there. Your life's an open book," he added with some amusement.

An open book? Not by a long shot. No one but her immediate family knew why her parents had hired a private tutor for her and why she'd concentrated so hard on her studies. Not even Ryan and Lily knew what had happened to her as a teenager, the wrong decisions she'd made and the foolish choices.

44

Rerouting the conversation back to her visit, she nodded to the letter in Peter's hand. "I'm here because Ryan asked me to speak to you."

"About?"

"He's having symptoms."

"What kind of symptoms?"

She took another paper from her purse, opened it and laid it on his desk. "First of all, I need to tell you that Lily knows nothing about this and that's the way Ryan wants it. That's also why he called me. He began having severe headaches and he didn't want to consult with a doctor in Red Rock or San Antonio because he tried to brush off the pain at first. He also didn't want any more rumors to get started. There have been enough about him concerning…everything."

"He's not still a suspect in the Christopher Jamison murder, is he? The police certainly should have ruled him out by now."

It sounded as if Peter had no doubts about Ryan's innocence. "Apparently they *haven't* ruled him out. That stress alone could cause headaches. But he told me he'd never had this type of headache before, so I took him seriously. I needed a vacation so I decided what better place to take it than in Red Rock."

"Are you staying at the Double Crown?"

"No, I'm staying with Miles and Clyde at the Flying Aces. I can't show too much concern about Ryan because Lily will become suspicious."

Peter took the evaluation she'd typed up then looked it over. His expression became more somber as he did. "He's having some tingling in his arm?"

"Yes."

"You said he didn't want to see anyone local. Why come to me when my speciality is pediatric neuro-surgery?"

"He trusts you, Dr. Clark. You'll keep all this confidential, including my involvement. I've recommended he have testing done but I'm not licensed to practice in Texas and I don't have hospital privileges here. You, however, do. Ryan thought if the two of us worked together, we could get to the bottom of whatever is wrong. It would safeguard his privacy."

After a second look at the report she'd written, Peter's gaze met hers. "I want to talk to Ryan myself."

"He'd rather not come here, and he doesn't want Lily or anyone else in the family to know."

When Peter rubbed his chin thoughtfully, Violet couldn't help but notice what a strong jawline he had, what large strong hands. "All right. I'm glad Ryan believes he can trust me. We can meet at my house. I can examine him and then we can decide what to do next."

"When are you available?" Violet asked.

"Tonight."

Obviously Peter Clark didn't like Ryan's symptoms any more than she did. "I'll call Ryan and see if he's free."

She took her little blue cell phone from her purse. A few minutes later, after a brief conversation with Ryan in which they all agreed on a time, she closed the phone and dropped it back into her purse.

"Ryan said to make sure to tell you he'll pay you double your usual fee because he knows this is an inconvenience."

"Ryan's a friend. There won't be a fee, not for tonight."

"He won't like that."

Peter smiled. "Maybe not, but it will be my only condition for examining him."

"I can see why he respects you," she said softly.

Silent communication passed between them and because of their concern for Ryan, a bond was formed. However, that bond seemed to be more personal than professional.

Standing, she met his gaze. "It was good to meet you, Dr. Clark. I don't want to take up any more of your time."

"It's Peter," he corrected her.

"Peter," she murmured.

Holding her gaze, he seemed to be waiting for something. Finally, with a wry smile turning up the corners of his lips, he asked, "And should I call you Dr. Fortune or Violet?"

She felt her cheeks turn hot and couldn't remember the last time she'd blushed. "Violet's fine," she decided, feeling much too warm in the small office.

When he stood and came around the desk, they were standing very close. "Ryan is lucky to have you in the family."

"He and my dad have always been close. I grew up respecting him, and he's like a favorite uncle. I don't want anything to happen to him."

"This could be serious."

She already knew that, the possibilities having kept her awake the past few nights. Still, she realized Peter felt he had to put the probability into words, so that she could take it as a warning, so that she wouldn't deny what might be the cause of Ryan's problems. "I know this could be serious. But on the other hand, stress and tension could cause symptoms, too."

"That's possible. We'll proceed one step at a time."

Feeling as if she could stand there all day just

looking at Peter, absorbing his strength, his concern and his compassion, she gave herself a mental shake. She didn't need any of those things from him. Ryan did.

With a deep breath, she stepped away from Peter's powerful aura and walked toward the door. "You don't have to see me out. Ryan says he knows where your house is located, so I guess I'll see you tonight."

"Tonight," Peter agreed, his deep voice making the word sound like a commitment.

As Violet escaped into the hall and closed Dr. Peter Clark's office door behind her, she knew it was a commitment to Ryan Fortune.

...NOT THE END...

48 *Look for* The Good Doctor *by Karen Rose Smith in stores October 2005.* ✒

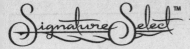

Signature Select™

THE
F RTUNES
OF TEXAS™:
Reunion

Coming in October...

The Good Doctor

by *USA TODAY* bestselling author

KAREN ROSE SMITH

Peter Clark would never describe himself as a jaw-dropping catch, despite being one of San Antonio's most respected neurosurgeons. So why is beautiful New York neurologist Violet Fortune looking at him as if she would like to show him her bedside manner?

Silhouette®
Where love comes alive™

Signature Select™

SAGA

National bestselling author
Debra Webb

A decades-old secret threatens to bring
down Chicago's elite Colby Agency in
this brand-new, longer-length novel.

COLBY CONSPIRACY

While working to uncover the truth behind
a murder linked to the agency, Daniel Marks
and Emily Hastings find themselves trapped
by the dangers of desire—knowing every
move they make could be their last....

Available in October,
wherever books
are sold.

Bonus Features
include:

Author's Journal,
Travel Tale
and
a Bonus Read.

Silhouette®
Where love comes alive™

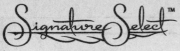

SPOTLIGHT

"Delightful and delicious...Cindi Myers always satisfies!"
—*USA TODAY bestselling author Julie Ortolon*

National bestselling author

Cindi Myers

She's got more than it takes for
the six o'clock news...

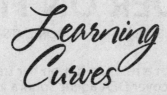

Learning Curves

Tired of battling the image problems that her
size-twelve curves cause with her network news
job, Shelly Piper takes a position as co-anchor on
public television with Jack Halloran. But as they
work together on down-and-dirty hard-news
stories, all Shelly can think of is Jack!

Plus, exclusive bonus features inside!

On sale in October.

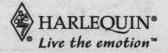

HARLEQUIN®
Live the emotion™